Alan Gibbons is a primary school teacher and started writing children's books in 1990. His central themes come from his own experience, and observation of children. Alan Gibbons lives in Liverpool with his wife and four children. One of his other books, *Shadow of the Minotaur,* won the Blue Peter Award in the 'Book I Couldn't Put Down' category, and was also shortlisted for the Carnegie Medal.

Julie and Me . . . and Michael Owen Makes Three

Alan Gibbons

TED SMART

First published in Great Britain in 2001
as a Dolphin paperback
by Orion Children's Books
a division of the Orion Publishing Group Ltd
Orion House
5 Upper St Martin's Lane
London WC2H 9EA

This edition produced for
The Book People Ltd
Hall Wood Avenue,
Haydock,
St Helens WA11 9UL

Reprinted 2001

A catalogue record for this book is available
from the British Library.

Typeset at The Spartan Press Ltd,
Lymington, Hants
Printed in Great Britain by
Clays Ltd, St Ives plc

ISBN 1 84255 048 9

For all at Prescot County Primary,
an inspirational school

PART ONE

Mad About the Girl
or
Phil Neville's Lunge

1

'Who's that?'

What's that might have been a better way of putting it. What I'm looking at is not so much a girl as a creature from another world. It's as though I've just been born again and suddenly I know what life is for.

'Who *is* that?'

My question is directed at my best mate Bobby Quinn. The way I say it makes his head snap round. I've gone all gaspy and urgent and breathless and he wants to know why. Probably thinks I've plugged myself into the electric mains or something. He joins me staring through the little oblong window in the sports hall door.

'Which one?'

What does he mean, which one? That one. The one with the hair and the shape and the grace.

The one.

'Over there, in blue.'

'Oh her. That's Julie Carter. She's new. She's in my maths set.'

That does it, I've got to work harder in maths! I'm in the second set. Bobby's in top . . . with Julie.

'Where's she from?'

Spirited from Wonderland . . . wafted here from Paradise . . . newly materialised from the planet Wow?

'Huyton. Just moved up from Page Moss.'

'You seem to know a lot about her,' I say, my eyes narrowing with suspicion. I don't believe it, I only saw her for the first time a minute ago and I'm jealous already.

3

'I talk to people,' says Bobby with a shrug. '*I'm* sociable.'

'*I* can be sociable,' I protest.

No, scrub that. I can't. I've never been more than a couple of steps above the hard core nerds. I'm often awkward talking to the other lads in my year, but with girls I'm completely tongue-tied and hopeless. I heard somewhere that the average tongue weighs six ounces – from Bobby probably. He's a mine of useless information. So if your average tongue weighs in at a bantamweight six ounces, how come mine swells to a mouth-clogging, word-dumbing, heavyweight ten pounds? It's like talking with a boa constrictor in your mouth.

'Fancy her, do you?' Bobby asks.

Fancy her?

Fancy her!

That's not the word for what I'm feeling. It doesn't even come close. My skin has gone hot and prickly. My heart is break-dancing in my ribcage. My mouth is as dry as sandpaper. I'm Mount Vesuvius and molten lava is surging up my oesophagus. What's more, for the first time in my life I actually understand what people mean when they say they've got butterflies in their tummy. Butterflies! What I've got is a swarm of enraged hornets.

'Why don't you ask her out?'

I stare at Bobby. Doesn't he understand what he's saying? Ask her out! This vision in blue. It takes me all my time to ask a girl to pass the salt in the canteen. So how exactly do I go about asking somebody as amazing as Julie to go out with me? She isn't just *a* girl. Suddenly, she's *all* girls.

'I couldn't.'

'Course you could. She's only a girl.'

Only!

It's all right for Bobby. He must have kissed the Blarney stone when he was little. No, he swallowed the thing whole. He could charm a fish out of the sea, could Bobby. He's popular with everybody; the teachers, the other boys, even the girls. He asked Caitlin Brady out at the end of last term. I watched him do it. He just marched up to her and popped the question. She's good-looking too. Not one of your needy, desperate girls. She agreed right away. They've been going steady ever since.

4

He doesn't seem to have any problem chatting up girls. He calls it the Nike technique. Just do it. And if they say no – what the heck – there are plenty more fish in the sea. Their loss, that's Bobby's philosophy. He's got self-confidence to burn.

'She wouldn't give me a second glance,' I stammer. 'I mean, just look at her.'

Bobby looks. 'Yeah, she's nice.'

Nice!

She's gorgeous.

For starters, she's tall. Oh my God, she's probably taller than I am, and what girl wants to be seen out with a midget? I can actually feel myself shrinking as I stand here. She's not skinny, though. No way, she's curvy. Sturdy-looking. Do you say that about girls, sturdy? Listen to me, will you, when it comes to the dating game I don't even know the vocabulary. She's – what's the right word? – sleek. Yes, that's spot on. Julie Carter is sleek. Tall, curvy, athletic and *sleek*. Then there's her hair. It's long and black and glossy. She's got it in one long braid down her back and it skips and jumps as she runs down the crash mat. Look at her, you can see every muscle moving in her legs. She's amazing.

'You have got it bad, haven't you?'

Bobby's right there. I've never felt anything like this. Except maybe that May night in Barcelona when Peter Schmeichel lifted the Champions League trophy and sealed the treble. That was the same sort of thrill. The feeling that makes you clench your fists and yell: Yiss!

But this is different. That was about Man U. fans everywhere. I was sharing something magical with millions of others across the world. But this surge of electricity, it's all about me. Me and Julie C. I watch her in her royal blue leotard and matching shorts and it's like she's there in a spotlight going through her routine just for me. Then this nagging thought comes knocking on my brain door. What about her personality? What if I pluck up the courage to talk to her and I don't like her. Think of it, she could be Miss Universe on the outside and the Wicked Witch of the East on the inside! A bit like the women on *Jerry Springer*. Oh no, don't tell me she's a bimbo. What if Julie's trailer trash?

5

'What's she like to talk to?'

Let her be nice, let her be nice, let her be nice.

'I like her.'

Yes!

'She's really friendly. She's dead popular already. I've never seen a new kid make friends so quickly.'

I press my nose against the window, my breath clouding the glass and almost obscuring my view of her doing a handstand, then gliding effortlessly into a perfect forward roll. Bobby brings me back to earth with a playful thump on the arm.

'Terry, I know you're head over heels in love and all that, but can we get to English? Spotty doesn't like you being late.'

He's right. Mr Spottiswood is the strictest teacher on the staff. Reluctantly, I start to detach myself from the window. That's when it happens. Julie pads to her Reebok sports bag and pulls out, of all things, a Liverpool shirt. I go through agonies as she slips it over her head. How can this be happening to me? Here I am watching the girl of my dreams and she's wearing the colours of our arch-enemies, the evil empire at the opposite end of the East Lancashire Road, Liverpool FC.

'Something wrong?' asks Bobby.

'Uh huh,' I tell him. 'Everything. She's only a Liverpool fan.'

Bobby shrugs.

'Never stopped me. I've been out with two Liverpudlians and I'm an Evertonian. I've even been out with one girl who didn't like football.'

We move along the corridor.

'Hurry up,' says Bobby. 'Your mind's still in the gym.'

He's right, it's up there hanging on the wall bars, transfixed by Julie Carter. Luckily, we beat Spotty to class. Just. That's when Bobby comes out with one of his famous useless facts:

'Do you know where the word gymnasium comes from?'

'No.'

'It's Greek. A place where you exercise naked.'

My mind falls off the wall bars. Bobby gives me a funny look.

'Terry, are you sweating?'

Sweating? It's a wonder I haven't had a heart attack!

Tuesday, 20th June
3.10 p.m.

The build-up starts here. No homework tonight, I've cleared the decks so that I can watch every second of studio discussion, every instant of the live match action.

England v. Romania.

The last group match of Euro 2000. Win or draw and we're through to the quarter-finals to play Italy. Lose and it's just the latest in the line of Great English Disasters.

'That's all we've got to do,' I remind Bobby, as if he needs reminding. 'Avoid defeat and we're through.'

'Piece of cake,' says Bobby. 'Though the Azurri will be tougher.'

'I'm not so sure Romania will be that easy,' I say. 'They beat us in the World Cup, remember.'

'Only because of that plank Le Saux,' says Bobby. 'Petrescu did him for pace and strength. Can't trust a Southerner to get anything right.'

I smile. He's right. Whoever heard of a footballer from the Channel Islands? Phil Neville's a good Northern lad. He'll show him how it's done.

'Want to come round to ours to watch it?' I ask. 'You can have your tea first if you like.'

'Don't mind if I do,' says Bobby. 'I'll just phone Mum and let her know.'

So there's Bobby on his mobile and me waiting for him by the school gates when Julie walks past with Kelly Magee. Bobby says Kelly's the spitting image of Sabrina, the Teenage Witch, but I think he's exaggerating. In her bad moments she looks more like Salem, the cat. If you ask me, even in her best clothes and fully made up she doesn't register above seven on the cuteness scale. Bobby probably fancies her. Let's face it, he fancies just about anything in a skirt. Now Julie, she's a definite ten. She even looks good in her school uniform. I ask you, green blazer and tie, blue jumper and skirt and she still looks good.

I find myself staring at her sports bag. The Liverpool shirt is hanging out of the top. It's like a red rag to this particular bull. I mean, football is the lens through which I see the world.

'What're you staring at?' asks Kelly.

'N-nothing,' I stammer, caught in the act.

I look all round me, as if my eyes alighted on Julie for just one nanosecond, purely by chance.

'He was staring at you, Julie.'

There's no conning Kelly. She's been out with more boys than I've had bacon toasties and she knows all the tricks. She flounces by, her eyes raking me with invisible fire. Julie doesn't even give me a second look. She must be used to boys staring.

'Weirdo,' observes Kelly. 'Freak-a-zoid.'

Julie doesn't say a word.

'Made the first move already, have you?' says Bobby as he slips his mobile away. 'You dirty dog. Quick off the blocks this time, eh?'

'Let's go,' I say, ignoring him.

'Put your tongue back in,' says Bobby before coming out with one of his famous useless facts: 'Did you know that by the age of twelve months you've dribbled one hundred and forty five litres of saliva?'

He looks at Julie. 'Mind you, anybody would find Julie Carter mouth-watering.'

I look away. I know I've gone bright red, the colour of that stinking Liverpool shirt.

Tuesday 20th June
7.30 p.m.

Something's up. There's definitely an atmosphere. Bobby's noticed it too. While we were having our tea, Dad said something under his breath to Mum about having a house meeting soon.

House meeting?

What's that about? We're not *Guardian* readers. We don't have house meetings. Who does he think we are, characters in some divvy sit-com? Ever since he mentioned the house meeting Mum has been stamping round slamming cupboards and plonking down cups. For a while I thought it was this new cabbage diet she's been on, but it's more than that. She isn't a happy bunny.

'Should I go?' Bobby asks just before kick-off.

Even somebody as thick-skinned as our Mr Bubbly is feeling uncomfortable.

'Don't be daft,' I tell him. 'It'll blow over. It always does. Besides, you'd miss the action.'

'So who's going to be the match-winner?' asks Dad, flopping into his armchair with a bottle of Stella. He's wearing the United away strip for the game so it's obvious what he expects to hear.

'Beckham,' says Bobby, 'Everything comes from his crosses.'

'Scholes,' I say. 'Watch his runs from deep.'

But it isn't either of the United players who catch the eye early on. Or even an Englishman. The Romanians are playing a fluent game of pass and move and within two minutes Ilie cracks a free kick round the wall. Nigel Martyn does well to stop Moldovan's shot. Bobby, Dad and I exchange worried looks. It isn't going according to plan. Twenty-two minutes into the match things are going from bad to worse. Chivu tries a chipped cross and it clears Martyn and bounces in off the upright.

We're 1–0 down.

'Not again,' groans Dad. 'They're going to throw it away as usual.'

Bobby gives me a meaningful look.

'Why are Dads always so negative?' he whispers.

'It's genetic,' I whisper back. 'They've got a whinging gene.'

'We'll get back into it, Mr Payne,' says Bobby.

He's right. Five minutes before the interval Paul Ince is brought down in the box.

'Ex-Man U,' I point out proudly. I conveniently forget that he's also ex-Liverpool.

Shearer sends the keeper the wrong way and me and Bobby are skidding across the wooden floor on our knees, arms raised in celebration. Then, in first-half injury time, a touch from Ince followed by the deftest of flicks from Paul Scholes puts Michael Owen through.

He uses his pace to get clear of the advancing keeper and slots the ball into the net. It doesn't get any better than this.

'Told you Scholes would do it,' I yell, bouncing up and down on the couch.

'Owen was the one who scored, you know,' Bobby points out.

'The hard work was already done by then,' says Dad.

He never was one to give a Liverpool player credit if he could help it. I wonder what Julie would make of the scene.

During the half-time break we're eating Kit-Kats. Mum's sadly munching an apple. She's sworn off chocolate. Something to do with the size of her love handles. We keep reading the scoreline. We can hardly believe our luck.

'Romania have played us off the park,' says Dad, 'And we're 2–1 up.'

'Just got to hold on to it now,' says Bobby. 'We were two up against Portugal and we still lost.'

'Not this time,' says Dad. 'You're going to see the old bulldog spirit come through.'

But there isn't much bulldog spirit on show after the break. The game has hardly restarted when Martyn punches the ball out to Munteanu. The Romanian chests it down and volleys it into the net. It's 2–2 and we're gutted. It doesn't get any worse than this.

'See how Martyn flapped at that?" says Bobby.

'Typical Leeds player,' snorts Dad, a bit unfairly I reckon.

'How much longer's this on?' moans Amy, my little sister, as she puts in an appearance in her Mulan nightie, the one she got in Florida.

'Ages,' I tell her, waving her out of the way of the screen.

For the rest of the match we're on the edge of our seats. Romania are pressing forward all the time. Their passing is neater and crisper than ours. But if we can only hold on . . .

'We're defending too deep,' says Dad. 'We're asking for it.'

And we get it.

'Two minutes left,' says Dad. 'Just two minutes. Come on, lads. Dig in.'

'Come on,' I say.

'Come on,' Bobby echoes desperately.

Somehow we all know what's coming. It's like destiny. A locomotive called defeat. But with the seconds ticking away we start to hope.

'Blow, ref,' pleads Dad.

Then the sky caves in. Moldovan drives into the penalty box. Phil Neville is challenging him all the way. Then the ex-Coventry man is past Phil on the outside.

'Stick to him,' I yell.

'But don't bring him . . .'

Phil lunges and flattens Moldovan.

'. . . down,' groans Bobby.

'He dived,' I cry, jumping to my feet in outrage as the ref points to the spot. 'Blatant dive. That Moldovan was the same when he played in the Premiership. Phil got a definite touch on the ball.'

Dad shakes his head. 'Not this time, Terry. The ref's got it right. It's a penalty.'

I remember Euro 96. Not penalties again. Not this.

Bobby covers his face with a cushion.

'I can't look,' he says.

I look and I wish I hadn't. Ganea converts from the spot. Agonising moments later it's full time. England 2, Romania 3.

I'm hollow, like somebody's shoved a pipe down my throat and hoovered out my insides. 'It's David Beckham all over again,' says Dad. 'The Man U-haters will be lining up to have a go.'

I remember the way Beckham kicked out in the World Cup game against Argentina and wince. Opposition fans booed Beckham for two years because of his red card. United were hated even more than usual. I took a lot of stick for Becks' rush of blood.

'Phil Neville's going to pay for that blunder.'

I think of all the anti-United feeling at school and Julie in her Liverpool shirt. Phil Neville isn't the only one who's going to suffer.

Bobby's gone home and Amy's tucked up in bed, so it's just me, Mum and Dad. We've been raking over the ashes of defeat for half an hour now, getting more and more down in the dumps. Even Mum, who doesn't have much of an interest in the beautiful game, is affected by it. The post-mortem is even more painful than usual after an England failure. Dad's ranting about Kevin Keegan like it's personal, and he's taking Phil Neville's mistake really badly, going on about how he's never going to be able to hold his head up at work.

'All those Scousers just waiting to take a rise out of me.'

After a while I start to wonder whether all this hot air really is about football. It's as if football's just the excuse, something to hang his rage on. Something's scratching away at the back of my mind, something about . . . yes, a house meeting.

'What's this house meeting anyway?' I ask, never dreaming I'm opening up a can of giant worms.

'Not now, eh, Geoff?' says Mum, a pleading look in her eyes. 'Surely it can wait until you're in a better mood.'

'Better mood,' snaps Dad. 'That's a good one.'

I'm starting to get worried. They've never been much for arguments, my parents. They usually show all the passion of a deep-frozen cod. But tonight I can almost touch the suppressed rage crackling between them.

'May as well know now as later,' grunts Dad. 'The lad's fifteen. It's not like anything's going to change. We'd just be putting it off.'

He's got this wild look in his eyes as though he wants to hurt everybody, especially himself. All of a sudden I'm not just worried, I'm scared.

'Geoff,' said Mum, panicky and anxious, 'don't say something you'll regret.'

But the wildness has got hold of Dad. He's in full flow.

'England throw it away again . . . lousy job . . . dead end life . . . all I do is work and what do I get for it? No thanks . . . feel like chucking it.'

'Dad, what are you on about?'

'Shall I tell him what I'm on about, Sharon?' he demands, eyes wilder than ever.

That seals it. This isn't about England. Even thirty years of hurt couldn't get him in this state. No, it's something else. I can feel the earth slipping away from under my feet.

'I'm moving out Terry, that's what I'm on about. I'm getting my own place.'

That can of worms, the creatures are all the size of anacondas with teeth like vampires.

'Geoff!' cries Mum. 'Not like this.'

The giant worms are chewing through my heart, ventricle by shredded ventricle.

'We've talked about how we'd tell the children.'

I can just imagine it. I've read about it in Mum's magazines when I was hunting for the naughty bits on the agony aunt pages: *It's your partner you're splitting up from, not your children.*

Well, wrong. I know exactly who Dad's splitting up from. All of us. I've read the little guides. *How to explain it to the kids. Letting them down gently.*

Well, believe me, there's nothing gentle about the way Dad's let me down. I feel like I've been run over by a lorry. This has come right out of the blue. Where were the quarrels, the raised voices, the thrown crockery, the slammed doors? Dad, where were the warnings?

'We've been drifting apart for a while,' says Mum, trying to salvage something after the explosion. 'It's not your fault, Terry.'

Not my fault. Well, duh! I *know* it's not my fault. It's yours, you pair of lousy fakes, pretending to be a couple when all the while you were planning to chuck your marriage in the bin.

'How long have you known? I ask. 'How long have you had this planned?'

'A couple of weeks,' says Dad. 'Well, a month or two actually.'

The bombshell explodes in my head. This has been going on since Easter at least.

'A month or two!'

All the things we've done in that time flash through my mind. Parents' evening, they were both at that. Mr and Mrs

Supportive. The day out at Alton Towers. Swimming at Heatwaves. Amy's birthday party. I see it all in freeze-frame. Me and Amy grinning our stupid heads off and all the time our family was a big, fat, lousy lie. Happy families, happy rotten families.

'I'm going to bed,' I say, making for the door.

I don't even want to look at them.

'No, Terry, not like this,' says Mum. 'Sit down for a couple of minutes.'

'Why?' I ask. 'Is Dad going to change his mind?'

Dad shakes his head. He's got this weird look on his face, like the guy who's let the evil genie out of the bottle and can't find the cork.

'Then I'm going to bed.'

Tuesday 20th June
11.30 p.m.

Today's a day I won't forget in a hurry.

When I saw Julie in the gym it was like conquering Everest. The feeling I had, it was like I just couldn't get any higher. But there's something they don't tell you about getting to the top of the mountain. From then on, the only way is down.

And boy, did I choose the quickest way to descend! The key moments flash through my mind as I fall.

Nigel Martyn flapping that cross . . .

. . . punching the ball to Munteanu . . .

. . . Phil Neville bringing down Moldovan . . .

. . . Alan Shearer crying.

The air is rushing more quickly. More moments:

. . . Dad ranting and raving at the TV . . .

. . . Mum with her pleading eyes . . .

. . . Dad saying it's over.

20th June 2000: the best of days, the worst of days.

2

To understand how I'm feeling as I trudge towards the school gates, you'll need to know something about Knowsley Manor High. The school is in Prescot on the eastern edge of Liverpool. The town is at the top of a long hill. At the bottom of the hill is Huyton where most of the kids come from. So what does that mean? I'll tell you what it means. Man U. fans are out-numbered about ten to one by Liverpudlians and Evertonians. We get more stick than a dog in the park. I missed Bobby this morning so into the valley of death trudged the one.

Here's what I hear as I reach the gates:

'I hear some plank of a Man U. player's sunk England again.'

The voice belongs to Fitz. That's John Fitzpatrick, my captain in the Year 10 football team. He's cock of the school. Bright, sporty, good with the girls. He seems to have been out with most of them. I've spent the last four years here trying to be just like him.

'What is it with you Mancs? First Beckham sabotages the World Cup for us, now Neville loses us Euro 2000.'

I'm trying to shrug it off. Dad was gone when I got up this morning and I'm in no mood for this. I'm all hot and red and my skin's prickling all over. Fitz knows he's getting to me.

'It wasn't Phil Neville's fault,' I retort.

'So whose was it?' asks Fitz with a mocking laugh. 'How did Romania get that penalty then, an act of God?'

I'm really starting to dislike Fitz. He's gone from role model to arch-enemy in ninety seconds.

What was I doing copying this Dingus Malingus?

15

'Martyn was to blame for the first two goals,' I say. 'And Paul Scholes set up Owen's goal, remember.'

I'm taking it too seriously. Why can't I just ignore him, let it roll over me the way Bobby does? I'll tell you why, Julie has put in an appearance and she's watching our argument with interest.

'Hey, Kelly, Julie,' says Fitz, 'Have you heard this one? He says it wasn't Neville's fault last night.'

'So whose fault was it?' asks Kelly Magee.

All these Scousers seem to be reading from a prepared script. I look into her Sabrina lookalike blue eyes and want to tell her where to get off. But she's Julie's new best mate so I keep my lip buttoned.

'He was unlucky,' I tell her.

'Unlucky! Is that what you call it?'

The three of them are laughing. At me. I can't stand to look at them, especially Julie. Why does she have to join in? But why shouldn't she? They're in the top maths set together and they all support Liverpool. I'm the odd one out here.

'Look at the state of him,' says John. 'I think he's going to cry.'

'Don't be stupid,' I retort. 'I didn't see any of your wonderful Liverpool players doing much either.'

'In case you didn't notice,' Julie says. 'Michael Owen scored.'

She says it matter-of-factly. There's no venom in her words.

'He took it brilliantly.'

'And he's gorgeous,' adds Kelly, sticking her unwanted oar in.

'Yes,' says Julie, acting all swoony. 'Definitely gorgeous.'

I look at her for the first time and suddenly I'm melting in those dark brown eyes. I like her and she likes Michael Owen. The eternal triangle.

'Yes,' I admit grudgingly. 'He took the goal well.'

'Now that's a first,' says Kelly. 'A Manc who admits he's wrong.'

'Bit like a Scouser who keeps her opinions to herself,' I snap back.

Me and my big mouth. I see Julie's heart-stopping eyes

narrowing. Congratulations Terry, you've just forced her even closer to the dreaded Fitz. Make a mental note: the girl you're mad about is a Scouser too. Now she's in a nark with you. What have I done? Quick, backtrack.

'I didn't mean all Scousers,' I stammer. 'I meant . . .'

'You don't know what you mean,' says Fitz, twisting the knife. 'Typical Manc. Anyway, I've got something for you.'

He's rummaging in his bag.

'It's here somewhere. I cut it out specially for you. Yes, here it is.' With a flourish, he produces a cutting from the *Mirror*. The headline pierces my heart. It consists of just one word: ROMANIAC!

'Wonder what United have got planned for the next World Cup,' Fitz muses. 'A Gary Neville own goal? You know, keep disaster in the family.'

With that they turn their backs and walk away. Not that I care about Fitz and Kelly. But the third back belongs to Julie and that hurts.

Wednesday 21st June
10.00 a.m.

Over half-way through double French and still no sign of Bobby. I decide to send him a text message: *Bobby, where are you? Terry.* The messages comes back a couple of minutes later:

What do you mean, where am I? Where are you?

Which sets off a hi-tech, low-sense exchange:

Me: *I'm in school, where do you think?*

Bobby: *School! What time is it?*

Me: *Ten o'clock, you dope.*

Bobby: *Ten o'clock! Ohmigod. Mum didn't get me up.*

Me: *You're lucky.*

Bobby: *Come again?*

Me: *My mum and dad have just split up.*

Bobby: *I'm in a rush. Give me the gory details when I get in.*

Get your skates on, Bobby lad. I think of Fitz and all the other Liverpudlians dying to take a pop at me. Something tells me I'll need all the friends I've got for morning break.

'Robert Quinn,' says Mrs Massie as he bursts through the door. 'What time do you call this?'

'Dix heures et demi,' Bobby answers in his best schoolboy French.

Mrs Massie doesn't see the joke.

'Have you been to the office to tell them you're in?'

'Yes.'

'And what cock and bull story did you give them?'

I can see Bobby biting his tongue. I know exactly what he'd say if he didn't stop himself: *Same cock and bull story I'm giving you.*

That's one of Bobby's problems. He always has to have the last word. Even if it's the wrong word. I've lost track of the times he's opened his mouth and put his size nine right in it.

'My asthma was bad, Miss. Did you know that by the age of twenty-one I will have breathed in enough air to inflate three-and-a-half million balloons?'

'Mm,' says Mrs Massie drily. 'And by the end of this lesson you will have breathed out enough hot air to fill the Goodyear airship.'

Our appreciative ripple of laughter is interrupted only by the bell for mid-morning break. As we elbow our way down the corridor Bobby gives me a sideways look.

'So what's with the Payne family this fine and sunny day?'

'Dad's gone.'

'Gone where exactly?'

'Dunno.'

'How come?'

I open my mouth to answer. Mum's got it into her head that it's because she's put on a bit of weight. If she could only squeeze into a size 12 she'd still have a marriage. Somehow, I don't think that's it. But that's when I realise, *I don't know.* I don't know why he's gone, or even where he's gone.

'He's just gone.'

'I didn't know your folks were having problems.'

'That's just it, Bobby, neither did I.'

18

We spill out of the side door and made for the far side of the yard overlooking the sports hall. I think briefly of Julie in a blue leotard, permit myself a dreamy smile, then glance at Bobby.

'He came out with it after the match. I think the Romania fiasco set him off.'

'First time I've heard of a footy divorce,' says Bobby.

I do my best to sound off-hand about it, but I don't think Bobby's fooled. He can see how cut up I am.

'No, I mean it's been building up and the match was the last straw. He said all sorts of weird stuff.'

'Like what?'

'I dunno. Like he hates his job.'

'Double-glazing fitter. Don't think I'd fancy it either. They're always knocking on our front door. Nobody wants it.'

'Plenty of people have got it. Come to think of it, you have.'

I realise we've got off the subject. Any time now Bobby will furnish me with a number of depressed double-glazing fitters in the greater Merseyside region.

'It isn't right, Bobby. It came right out of the blue.'

'Sounds like my first divorce,' says Bobby.

Of course, I'd clean forgotten. His mum has been married twice, first to the baldy chap from St Helens – Bobby's dad – then to the man with the squint and the budgie from West Kirby. Funny taste in men, Bobby's mum. At the moment she's going out with this bloke from round the corner. Big guy with a cocker spaniel. Long furry ears and a shiny nose. The spaniel, not the boyfriend.

'You didn't expect it, then?'

'No way, I was thunderstruck. That wasn't the worst thing though.'

Right now, I can't imagine anything worse than the split.

'So what was?'

Bobby taps his nose knowingly.

'Access days, Terry. Access days.'

'Go on.'

'Your dad comes round to take you out. You must have seen them in McDonalds, miserable-looking men with their sprogs shovelling chips and chicken nuggets. At weekends they take up half the tables. I call it Access Alley.'

I've got the picture firmly fixed in my mind. Access Alley: lose hope all ye who enter here.

'Oh.'

'Oh is right Terry lad. I mean, your bedroom can only take so many beanie babies and plastic Disney characters. They take you everywhere at first, Camelot, Blue Planet Aquarium, Chester Zoo, the cinema. It's the guilt, you see, quickest route to their pockets. Then they get their first post-separation bank statement. After a while it's take-away pizza and a walk in Taylor Park. But that's not the worst of it.'

'No?'

'Oh no. On the rainy days it's back to Dad's bedsit with a video of *The Little Vampire* and a KFC.'

He looks around furtively. He's enjoying this, initiating me into the terrors of marital meltdown.

'But you've still not hit rock bottom. You know what comes next?'

I hardly dare ask.

'No.'

'One day, one dreadful day you dad will turn round and ask: *So what do you want to do today?* He's all out of ideas. Either that, or he's just stopped caring. That's when you know your relationship has gone critical.'

'Oh, behave, Bobby,' I say.

'I'm not kidding,' he says. 'You know all that father-son bonding stuff? Forget it. I hardly see my old man now. Better that way, I suppose.'

I can tell by the look on his face he doesn't really mean it. There's a space in his heart that will forever be occupied by a baldy guy from St Helens.

'I know my dad, Bobby. He took me to the Champions League Final in Barcelona, remember. You don't do that if you don't care. It was the greatest day of my life. And we shared it. Me and my dad.'

The greatest day of my life. Rivalled only by the sight of Julie Carter in the sports hall.

'We go to Old Trafford together for every home game. It's the highlight of my week. None of that Access Alley stuff is ever going to happen to us.'

20

I can see the future stretching out before me, one long Sir Matt Busby Way, straight and true. The only difference is, Mum and Dad are on opposite pavements.

Bobby shakes his head slowly.

'You can't rely on anything once your parents separate. Things are going to change, Terry. They're going to change a lot.'

I can see Dad and myself walking down the Ramblas singing *Championes* and reliving Sheringham and Solskjaer's goals all the way back home to Prescot. Us end up as two sad lads eating chicken pieces in a bedsit?

Never.

Wednesday 21st June
1.15 p.m.

We're getting changed for football when Bobby drops his bombshell.

'You've got a rival for the lovely Julie's affections,' he tells me.

'Who?'

'Fitz.'

I look across at John Fitzpatrick. I thought he'd been hanging round her a lot.

'You know I was wondering how Julie got so popular in such a short space of time?' says Bobby.

'Uh huh.'

It's hard to reply properly with a lump in your throat.

'Well, it turns out she knew loads of the kids here even before she came to Knowsley Manor. They met at the gym club at the leisure centre.'

'Who did?'

'Julie, Kelly, Pepsey Cooper, Fitz . . .'

'Hang on a minute. Fitz does gymnastics?'

'No, you dope. His little sister does. It turns out old Fitzy's known Julie for the last six months, ever since his Hayley joined the gym club at the leisure centre. If you're going to make a move, you'd better do it sharpish. You know Fitz's reputation.'

Do I? Fitz has had loads of girlfriends. I mean, we're talking two figures. That's why they call him, Frisky Fitzy. Some say he's got a bit of a look of Michael Owen, which helps. Oh great, it'll really help with Julie. She's *mad* about Michael Owen. That love triangle's turned into a love quadrilateral. Bobby's about to go when something occurs to me.

'What *did* happen to you this morning?'

'You're not going to believe this,' says Bobby.

'Try me.'

'Mum thought I was staying at yours last night. She didn't see me come in. Too busy with lover boy.'

(That's the one with the spaniel.)

'So when she went out to work this morning she locked the house up. Only locked me inside, didn't she?'

Bobby's front door is a double-glazed unit with seven mortice locks. My dad fitted it cheap.

'So what did you do?'

'I couldn't find my keys. I only had to climb out of my bedroom window and shin down the drainpipe. Got some really funny looks from the neighbours.'

'Bobby,' I say, 'It could only happen to you.'

He shrugs in that *stuff happens* way of his.

'Anyway,' says Bobby, 'I've got to pee. See you out there.'

I watch Fitz lacing up his boots and suddenly I'm wondering where you can buy voodoo dolls with Michael Owen haircuts.

'Something the matter?' he asks, catching my eye.

'No, why?'

'Dunno, just thought you might want to apologise for Chopper Neville's act of madness.'

'Oh, let it drop.'

Fitz starts to clatter across the tiled floor on his new studs. I admire the boots but not the boy in them.

'What, and let a Manc off the hook? Never.'

I'm last out of the changing rooms. As I go to pull on my shirt I catch my reflection in the mirror. Milk-bottle skin, freckles, bony shoulders, untidy ginger hair and legs like matchstick. I have this recurring nightmare. I'm growing up to look like Chris Evans.

'Hey, carrot top,' shouts Fitz. 'We're waiting for you.'

I bite my lip. Julie and Fitz. No, not that. Anything but that.

Wednesday 21st June
1.45 p.m.

Fitz is laughing at me. He's done me twice for pace and his team is 2–0 up already. I've got a great football brain. It's the body that's the problem.

This was my last chance to impress Mr Shooter and get myself into the side for the Knowsley Boys' Cup Final. We're playing Blackridge on Monday after school. It's me or Chris Lawlor for the last midfield place.

'You'd better buck your ideas up,' says Bobby. 'Six Guns has got Chris pencilled in for Monday.'

Mr Shooter is making notes on the touch-line.

'I know. Fitz is doing this on purpose.'

'Then don't let him. Get tighter on him.'

Six Guns walks purposefully to the centre and gestures to the teams.

'Second half, lads. Ready?'

Fitz is doing hamstring stretches on the edge of the centre circle. Suddenly I'm seeing him in a new light. He isn't just into girls any more. He's into *my* girl. He really loves himself. I reckon lads like him must come in flat-packs. Construct-a-Creep.

'Psst,' hisses Bobby. 'Seen who's watching? They must have a free period.'

It's Kelly and Julie. That settles it. I'll get tight on Fitz all right. He isn't going to make a monkey out of me a third time. Jamie Sneddon picks up the ball and looks for Fitz. He's coming my way with his right arm raised.

I decide to close him down and get to the ball first, putting it into touch.

'More like it,' says Bobby.

I permit myself a smile. I hope Julie was watching. Ten minutes later Gary Tudor turns provider. Again I get in before Fitz, clearing the ball downfield. Paul Scully gets on to the end of it and pulls one back for us. 2–1 down. Now we can make a game of it. I can see Six Guns making notes. I'm not doing myself any harm at all. I wonder what Julie thinks. No, don't let your mind wander. Just stay focused, Terry lad.

No Phil Nevilles.

Five minutes from the end Paul gets on the wrong side of his defender and scores with a glancing header. We've pulled level, 2–2.

'No silly mistakes,' says Bobby, clapping his hands. 'Keep it tight lads.'

It's easier said than done. Fitz's team are pressing us back. I glance at my watch. Two minutes left. Just like last night. Keep your concentration, Terry lad.

No Phil Nevilles.

Then I hear Bobby screaming at me. Gary Tudor has played a long ball over the top and put Fitz clear. I scamper across to intercept the ball. He's in the penalty box. God, he's fast. Just like Michael Owen, low centre of gravity and lots of pace. He's weaving and doing step-overs as I go to meet him, then he pushes it ahead of him, trying to turn me. I'm dying to get a foot in. My every instinct is screaming *flatten him. Demolish the Knowsley Manor Casanova.*

But no, I can't do it.

No Phil Nevilles.

We're shoulder to shoulder. I'm determined to force him wide. That's when he taps the ball through my legs. The lousy rat's nutmegged me!

I try to get out of his way, but his pace takes him into me. We go down in a tangle of legs and arms. Fitz is up first, arms raised. I scramble up after him waving mine.

'No pen,' I cry. 'Accidental. He ran into me.'

But Six Guns is having none of it. He points straight to the spot. Penalty. Fitz walks up and strokes the ball in. I look over to the touchline. Kelly and Julie are clapping wildly. The next ninety seconds fly past. It's too late to equalise again. I look from Julie on the touchline to Six Guns making his notes. No way am I in the team.

I'm out of luck with both of them.

3

Six Guns finishes the register. He's our form teacher as well as head of PE. He's got these laser beam eyes that instantly lock on to trouble. He spends most of his time wandering round school in his tracksuit looking hard.

'There are still a few of you who haven't given me their preferences for work experience week. May I remind you that it starts in just over a fortnight. Michael Gavin?'

Michael approaches the desk and hands in his slip.

'What's this, lad?'

'It's what I want to do.'

'Poodle clipping?'

Loud guffaws from the scallies at the back.

'I like dogs.'

Six Guns rolls his eyes.

'Are you taking the Mickey, Mickey?'

'No, I really do like dogs.'

'Takes all sorts, I suppose.'

He inspects the crumpled slip.

'Where's this been?'

'My dog got it.'

Six Guns looks like he's about to self-destruct.

'Poodle?'

'Labrador.'

With a look of distaste Six Guns put the slip in a folder.

'John Fitzpatrick?'

I watch as Fitz hands in his slip.

'Pony sanctuary?' exclaims Six Guns. 'First dogs, now horses.

What do you lot think this is, the RSPCA? I didn't take you for an animal lover, Fitzpatrick.'

Bobby frowns. It's one of those long, purposeful frowns, the sort that usually signals heap big doo-doo hitting the fan.

'What did you put down?' I ask Bobby.

'Electrical engineering. It's what I want to do when I leave school. You?'

'Promise you won't laugh.'

'Sure, I promise.'

'Fitness industry.'

'You're kidding!'

'My cousin was taken on for a week at one of the big fitness clubs on the Wirral. It was a doss. All he had to do was polish a few machines and sort some paperwork. He spent all his time on the treadmill or in the jacuzzi.'

'You sure there isn't a hidden agenda in there somewhere?'

'Meaning?'

Bobby gives a knowing wink.

'Spend a week working out. Come back from work experience tanned and conditioned. Wow the lovely Julie with your pecs.'

I can just see us. Julie in her blue leotard. Me in my black Speedo trunks flexing my biceps.

'Don't be soft. I'd only be there a week.'

'So it hadn't crossed your mind?'

'Wouldn't say that,' I confess. 'I wouldn't mind a bit more muscle. The way I am at the moment I can't even fill my T-shirts.'

'That's because you're an ectomorph,' says Bobby.

'You're a flipping ectomorph!' I retort.

'No, it's your body shape, stupid, the physique you're born with. You're an ectomorph – lean and skinny.'

'Oh, what are you?'

'Endomorph – big and brawny.'

Make that little and brawny. I'm at least four inches taller than Bobby.

'Wish I was an endormorph,' I mutter, imagining myself in front of the mirror.

'Don't,' says Bobby. 'You can eat anything you like and still be thin. If I even look at a cream cake it's hello Pavarotti.'

I glance at Fitz, my rival in love.

'What's he then?'

'You don't want to know.'

'Bad news, is it?'

'The worst. John Fitzpatrick's got the look. He's a meso-morph – broad shoulders, thin waist and natural strength.'

'Lousy mesomorph,' I growl in my best Homer Simpson voice.

Bobby splutters out a laugh.

'Care to let us in on the joke, Mr Quinn?' drawls Six Guns.

'Sorry, Mr Shooter.'

Six Guns shoves back his chair. 'Off to classes, people.'

**Friday 23rd June
12 noon**

Bobby plonks his tray on the table and sits down opposite me.

'Pizza?' I say. 'Is that the right food for an endomorph?'

'No.'

'So why'd you get it?'

Bobby takes a huge bite.

'I like pizza.'

He wipes tomato gunge off his mouth.

'You're not going to like this,' he says.

My stomach lurches. I remember the way he frowned in class.

'Is this about Julie?'

Bobby nods.

'I've found out why Fitz is so keen on the pony sanctuary.'

'Go on.'

'Julie already has her placement, see. Guess where?'

'The pony sanctuary?'

'Got it in one. So the moment Frisky Fitzy gets wind of it, he puts in his own horsey little request. With his track record, I don't think he's developed an interest in animal welfare, if you get my drift. Listen to me Terry, you're going to blow this. Ask the girl out before he does.'

'I can't.'

'Why ever not?'

'She might turn me down.'

'So she turns you down,' says Bobby. 'You haven't lost anything, have you?'

I look over to the door where Julie has just walked in with Kelly.

'Course I would. I'd have lost Julie.'

Just then, we spot Bobby's girlfriend looking round the canteen for him.

'Caitlin,' shouts Bobby. 'Over here.'

Caitlin slides in next to him and whispers something in his ear. He laughs. Great, I'm playing gooseberry again. I had to stand for ten minutes at the top of an alleyway last week while they were snogging away.

'Caitlin,' says Bobby. 'You're a girl.'

'Hey, you noticed.'

'Terry here needs some advice.'

I give him a pleading look. Oh, come on Bobby, don't make a show of me.

'He's mad about Julie Carter. Think he's got a chance?'

'Dunno. Maybe. She's not going with anybody as far as I know.'

'What about Fitz?'

Caitlin wrinkles her nose. Suddenly I like her a whole lot more than I ever have before.

'I went out with him for a while. He was all right at first, then he showed his true colours. He's a creep. His rotten paws were all over me. It's like dating an octopus.'

Bobby leaps to his feet, brandishing what's left of his pizza like a sword.

'The bounder! I'll run him through with my rapier.'

'Sit down,' says Caitlin, smiling indulgently. 'Your rapier's gone limp.'

'Don't be so personal,' says Bobby. 'So you reckon Terry's got a chance?'

'You could give it a go,' says Caitlin, nonchalantly sipping her Diet Coke.

Only a cute girl who's already got a boyfriend could be so casual.

'My sentiments exactly,' says Bobby. 'There you have it, Terry. Straight from the horse's mouth.'

'Watch who you're calling a horse,' chuckles Caitlin.

'Anyway, got to scoot,' says Bobby. 'We've got double maths.'

I nod. He and Caitlin, Julie and Fitz are all in the top set. I really have got to work harder on my maths. I'm taking my tray back when I see Fitz make a beeline for Julie and Kelly. He's leaning over them, laughing like a hyena. Julie's laughing too. Caitlin's right. Fitz is a creep. I look at him with his wide shoulders, his thin waist and his Michael Owen haircut.

Lousy mesomorph!

Friday 23rd June
3.10 p.m.

I walk as far as the Fusilier with Bobby and Caitlin. They'll be turning left towards St Helens Road. I'll be going straight on.

'Well,' says Bobby as we pause outside the pub. 'Did you?'

'Did I what?'

'Ask her out?'

I shake my head.

So does Bobby.

'What's he like? Listen to your uncle Bobby. Either you ask the girl or you lose the girl. You've got to be Nike-ad man. Just do it.'

Easier just said than just done.

'I didn't get a chance.'

'Didn't get a chance? You've been in the same school as her all day, for pete's sake!'

'Kelly's always with her.'

'I don't notice Fitz letting that stop him. He just steams right in there.'

'That's different. He's . . .'

'What?'

'Confident, mouthy . . . mesomorphic.'

'Then get confident,' says Bobby. 'You'll kick yourself if you don't.'

Bobby and Caitlin set off up the road holding hands. He stops by the petrol station.

'Hey, are you coming down to the community centre tonight? The band are practising for the big gig.'

The band is *The Sons of Moe Szyslak* and Bobby's big gig is a fifteen-minute slot at the end of year school disco.

'Yes, I'll be there.'

Anything to take my mind off Julie Carter and Frisky Fitzy.

Friday 23rd June
3.45 p.m.

I hear the key in the door, then Mum and Amy's voices.

'Are you in yet, Terry?'

'I'm in my room.'

'Would you come down a minute?'

I find her in the kitchen, making Amy a sandwich. She looks harassed.

'Listen love, I've got a favour to ask.'

'Go on.'

'It's Amy. I wonder whether you could start picking her up from school. Karen's asked me if I'd like to work through until five-thirty instead of knocking off at three.'

Karen is Mum's boss at the hairdressers where she works.

'It's another seventy pounds a week. We could do with the money, what with your dad leaving. Well?'

'It'll be a bit of a rush.'

'No it won't. You get out at ten past and Amy doesn't get out until half past. A fit young lad like you can walk the distance in less than ten minutes. You've got plenty of time.'

'Do I have to?'

'Terry, things aren't easy just now. I thought you'd want to help. All I . . .'

OK, OK, enough with the emotional blackmail.

'I'll do it.'

'Sure?'

'I said I'll do it.'

'Good lad.'

She calls up to Amy.

'Amy, your sandwich is ready.'

Amy is already in her boots and riding hat. Friday night is horse-riding night. A mad rush to the stables just outside Kirkby.

'I've got some news for you,' says Mum. 'From now on Terry will be picking you up from school.'

Amy pouts. 'Why can't you do it?'

'I've got to work late.'

'Why?'

'I just have, that's all.'

'It's because of Dad, isn't it?'

'Well partly, yes. Oh, that's the other thing I've got to tell you. Your dad will be taking you out tomorrow.'

An electric shock fizzes through me. It's just like Bobby said.

'Is this an Access Day?' I ask.

'I never thought of it like that,' says Mum. 'But yes, in a way it is. I know you don't like the idea of Geoff moving out. He may have finished with me but he's still your dad. I'm sure he'll take you somewhere nice. McDonald's maybe.'

A vision of Access Alley flashes through my mind and I shudder.

'Something up, Terry?' asks Mum.

'No,' I tell her, images of Camelot and the Blue Planet Aquarium and seedy bedsits flashing through my brain. 'Somebody stood on my grave.'

Friday 23rd June
7.00 p.m.

I lean over to Caitlin and shout over the noise of the band.

'They're not bad at all.'

'I beg your pardon?'

I'm battling with Bobby's lead guitar.

'The band, they're not half bad.'

'No.'

Caitlin's no conversationalist. Bobby likes it that way. He does the talking for both of them. I move away again and listen to *The Sons of Moe Szyslak* racing through 'Heatwave.' Bobby likes all that eighties mod-revival stuff. The Jam, Elvis Costello, the Specials. He explained it to me. The Who, the Small Faces, first generation mod. The Jam, second generation mod. *The Sons of Moe Szyslak*, third generation mod. The frenetic pace appeals to him. That's the way he wants to live his life. He says his dad, the baldy chap from St Helens, was a rude boy when he was young. Do they have rude boys in St Helens, I ask myself?

Anyway, the St Helens rude boy gave Bobby two guitars, an acoustic and an electric lead guitar, just before he cleared off. The electric one is signed by Paul Weller, whoever he is.

'The next song,' says Bobby, 'is "Alison" by Elvis Costello. It's for my best friend Terry. I just hope he gets his Alison.'

He winks at me. Even though there are only the four members of the band, Caitlin, me and the caretaker in the building, I blush right to the tips of my ears. Bobby can be a real wuss sometimes. When they finish their set I collar him.

'Knock it off, will you?'

'What?'

'Stop broadcasting to the world that I fancy Julie Carter.'

'You do, don't you?'

'You know I do.'

'Then stop whingeing. I'm only trying to help.'

'I don't need your help.'

'You need somebody's.'

'Meaning?'

'Meaning there's no point moping around making cow eyes. You've got to go up to her and ask her out.'

By the time he's finished he's almost shouting.

'I'll get round to it in my own good time,' I tell him.

'Then heaven help you,' Bobby replies.

'What's what supposed to mean?'

'In a fortnight we start work experience. Now I'm thinking Frisky Fitzy has got a pretty good chance of getting in at the pony sanctuary. I'm thinking barns, rolls in the hay, get my drift?'

I do. All of a sudden I wish Bobby didn't paint quite such a vivid picture.

'So you're going to ask her out?'

'Yes.'

'When?'
'Monday.'
'Definitely?'
'Definitely.'
Well, maybe definitely.

4

It's Camelot.

As we queue up to pay for our tickets Amy squeals with joy. It's her favourite theme park, except for Disney of course, but she knows that holiday eighteen months ago was a once in a lifetime thing. I watch a cloud shaped like Fitz float overhead and remember Bobby's prophecy. Welcome to Access Alley.

'What do we go on first?' asks Dad.

He's never been before. It always used to be Mum who took us to theme parks. He takes me to Old Trafford. Everything else he seems to wriggle out of. Mum's always been the Family Entertainments Officer, parks, swimming baths, amusement parks, that sort of stuff.

'Log flume,' shouts Amy. 'Log flume, log flume, log flume.'

'Just so long as I don't get wet,' says Dad. 'This shirt's a brand new Ben Sherman.'

'Oh, we won't get wet, will we Terry?' says Amy, thinking it's a great joke.

I shake my head indifferently. As we walk away from the log flume I note with satisfaction that Dad is soaked through right down to his Calvin Klein boxers. Serves him right for busting up the family.

'What's next?' asks Dad. 'Just remember my stomach. I'll go on anything just so long as it doesn't go upside down.'

'Then it's got to be Excalibur,' I say, winking at Amy.

As we walk away from Excalibur I grin triumphantly. The sight of Dad suspended upside down high above the

34

Lancashire countryside with a stricken look in his eyes gives me a special pleasure. Take that, home-wrecker!

'Come on, kids,' says Dad. 'Joke over. No more upside-downers, OK?'

'No more upside-downers,' giggles Amy.

We exchange glances.

'Tower of Terror,' we shout with one voice.

As we walk away from the Tower of Terror Dad is definitely green round the gills.

'What did you have for breakfast?' I ask him.

Before he has a chance to answer I add: 'Don't worry. I'll be finding out soon enough.'

'Very funny.'

I have absolutely no sympathy. He's the one who dragged us down Access Alley, so he's the one who's got to pay the price. We all have something different for dinner. Pizza for Amy, fish and chips for me, cheese and tomato roll for Dad. It's three lots of queuing, but what the heck, it's his treat.

'Having a good time, kids?' asks Dad.

'Yeah,' says Amy.

'Whatever,' I answer off-handedly.

He can't really think I'm going to be bought off with a day out at Camelot.

You owe us for what you've done, Dad.

You owe us big time.

Saturday 24th June
3.30 p.m.

I'm starting to go easy on Dad. He's tried his best all day. He's even been on the Tower of Terror three times without barfing. Besides, I've just noticed the time. In six or seven weeks about this time I'll be watching Ryan Giggs unlocking Newcastle United's defence. I glance at Dad. This is the man who takes me to the Theatre of Dreams week in, week out. And no matter what he's done since, we'll always have Barcelona.

'A couple more rides,' says Dad, 'Then we'll have to be making tracks. What'll it be, Amy?'

'Tower of . . .'

'Whoa there, I think I'm all terrored out. Isn't there a little ride you can go on by yourself? I want a chat with Terry. Boys' stuff.'

'I haven't been on the umbrellas yet.'

'Right, umbrellas it is.'

Dad watches Amy climbing skywards then turns to me.

'I know you must think I'm the bad guy in all this, Terry.'

I shrug.

'Your mum and I were childhood sweethearts,' he explains. 'She was my first girlfriend. It was great at first. I loved the bones of her. Still do in a way.'

He waves to Amy.

'But something's gone. I don't get the butterflies any more.'

I remember Julie in the blue leotard and I kind of know what he means about butterflies. I've got a non-stop fluttering inside.

'When you've been with the same person for twenty years you start asking yourself: is this all there is? I suppose I want to chat people up again. I want the thrill of the chase.'

'Da-ad.'

He's definitely sharing too much.

'Sorry son, but that's the way I feel. Life became so . . . samey. Same old routine, day in, day out. I want a bit of excitement.'

'And you can't have that with Mum?'

He shakes his head.

'She thinks you've left because she's put on weight,' I tell him. 'That's why you don't fancy her any more.'

'I wish it was that simple,' Dad replies. 'I just got bored, that's all. We started turning into each other. I got this feeling that, if I didn't get out from under, we'd wind up walking round Asda in matching pullovers.'

Somehow I didn't think that sounded so bad. I'd walk round Asda with Julie any day.

'What about us?' I ask, my mind still full of me and Julie in our matching pullovers.

'You know I'll always be around,' says Dad. 'My feelings for you and Amy will never change, you've got my word on that.'

I wonder about the promises he's made to Mum. All the *forevers* and *happy-ever-afterwards* that must have dropped from his lips over the years. Suddenly, nothing seems certain any more.

'We'll do this every weekend.'

'It's going to be a busy weekend,' I say.

'I beg your pardon?'

'The match, Dad. The match.'

Dad's been a season ticket holder since the seventies. He started taking me to Old Trafford in the 1992–3 season. I was only seven but I can remember every twist and turn. Our six defeats still hurt, but not enough to eclipse the twenty-four victories, including a 2–1 away win against Liverpool. What a first season that was. That was the year we signed Eric Cantona. It was also the year we won the League Championship, our first in twenty-six years.

'I've been meaning to talk to you about that, son.'

My heart lurches, but before I can ask him what he means Amy's ride finishes. By the look on Dad's face he's eternally grateful to the umbrella ride.

'Only one more, Amy love,' says Dad, glancing nervously at me, 'A quickie.'

She settles for the carousel.

'What did you mean by that?' I demand. 'About the match.'

Dad doesn't meet my eyes.

'We've got two households to run now, Terry. We're really strapped for cash.'

Not so strapped he isn't buying himself new clothes.

'So?'

'So I've had to let our season tickets go.'

A rush of horror corkscrews through me.

'You've done what!'

'I couldn't afford to renew them.'

'Oh Dad, tell me you're joking!'

'I was struggling to afford it last season,' he says hurriedly. 'It's an expensive day out, son, it really is. What with the separation, there's no way we can do it.'

All I can do is stand there, staring in disbelief. I see

Schmeichel turning a somersault, I see Fergie holding up the Champions League trophy, finally I see me and Dad dancing down the Ramblas singing *Championes* and suddenly it's all one big sick joke.

'Dad, how could you?'

Without another word, I turn on my heel and walk away. I hear Dad yelling after me.

'Terry. *Terry!*'

Saturday 24th June
5.30 p.m.

On the way home Dad has his tapes on loud. I'm glad. I don't want to talk to the man who's just shut me out of the Theatre of Dreams. After the third play of 'Born to Run' by Bruce Springsteen Amy rebels.

'Can't we have the radio on?'

'Why?'

'Your stuff is so *old*.'

Dad pulls up outside the house but he leaves the engine running.

'Aren't you coming in?' asks Amy.

By now, Mum's on the doorstep, smiling thinly. She wraps her cardigan round her, as if trying to hide her belly.

'No, not tonight love. I've got to get off.'

As he pulls away I hear someone saying my name.

'Hi Terry.'

I turn to find myself looking right into Julie Carter's eyes. They're brown and bright. You'd almost think she was glad to see me.

'Oh hi, Julie.'

She's wearing a red and white Coq Sportif tracksuit. She looks cool and athletic. I'm aware that I'm sweaty and dishevelled after a hard day's roller-coastering. I see myself in her eyes, a scruffy, ginger dwarf. I shift awkwardly from right foot to left.

'What brings you up here?'

'I've been round at Kelly's all afternoon. She only lives up the road.'

'Oh yeah. Forgot.'

We look at each other. I'm dying to say something brilliantly witty. Dying to, but failing.

'Time to go home to my parents and the three stooges,' says Julie.

'Huh?'

'My kid brothers.'

'What are their names?'

'Guess.'

'Huey, Duey and Louis?'

Julie laughs, which comes as a surprise. The moment I say it I'm trying to swallow the words back into my mouth.

'Not far off. It's Gerard, Josh and John-Joe.'

I feel encouraged. I mean, here's Julie Carter, the *gorgeous* Julie Carter, laughing and joking with me and she isn't bored or anything. She isn't even fidgeting or looking around. She actually seems to be enjoying my company.

'So there are four of you: Gerard, Josh, John-Joe and Julie?'

'Mm, my Mum isn't very adventurous when it comes to consonants.'

I smile. Bobby was right. Julie is nice, and so easy to talk to. I don't feel tongue-tied at all. It would be no effort to ask her out right now. Do it, Terry, do it now. The words start to form in my mind.

'I'll have to run for my bus,' says Julie, glancing at her watch. 'See you in school on Monday. Kelly and I are going to watch you play Blackridge.'

Julie's thrown me off the scent. Don't let the moment pass, I tell myself, ask her. But I don't ask her. Instead I mumble something like:

'I'm only substitute. Fitz got past me too easily at practice.'

'I know,' said Julie. 'He's really good, isn't he?'

What have I done? Instead of asking her out, I've only reminded her that Frisky Fitzy is better than me! Just as I'm trying to salvage something, Amy appears at the door.

'Hurry up, Terry. Mum says tea's on the table.'

'Got to go,' I mutter.

'Yes, me too,' says Julie. 'If I miss my bus it'll be twenty minutes until the next one. It was nice talking to you, Terry. Bye.'

'Bye.'

I watch her walking briskly away, her plait bobbing.

5

'Terry,' says Bobby, 'you're one seriously sad little man.'

I look down at my feet like a kid getting told off.

'Just think about it. Destiny handed you the best chance you're ever going to get with Julie, and you passed up on it.'

'I got interrupted.'

'Do you want to know what you say the next time your sister interrupts you? Remember these immortal words, Terry: *Don't butt in, butt out.*'

'It sounds easy when you say it.'

Bobby sucks in his breath. He's getting frustrated with me.

'Terry, it *is* easy. You had Julie on her own. What does it take with you, a written invitation?'

'You weren't there. You don't understand.'

'Terry, *she* came up to you. *She* spoke first. *She* told jokes. Listen to me, because I'm only going to say it once: *She likes you, you big dope.*'

I catch my reflection in the long, black drama department window. What I see resembles a uniform hanging from a yard brush, topped with fluffy, flyaway ginger hair. A babe magnet I'm not.

'I don't know.'

Bobby leads the way into school, shaking his head. We make our way to our desks, but before Bobby has the chance to continue his interrogation in walks Six Guns.

'Good morning,' he says gruffly.

'Good morning, sir.'

Bobby digs me in the ribs.

41

'Look, he's got our placements.'

I strain to read the list on Six Gun's clipboard. Sure enough, it's headed *Work Experience*. Six Guns takes the register then starts down his list.

'I'm afraid we couldn't place you all with your first choices,' he begins. 'Bobby Quinn, you're working at Lewis's.'

'Lewis's,' said Bobby. 'But that's a department store. What's that got to do with electrical engineering?'

'Maybe they'll let you change a light bulb.'

The comment draws loud laughter from the back.

'Michael Gavin, you'll be happy. You're at the Pooch Parlour in Bootle.'

Michael – now known as Mick the Dog – looks so happy I expect to see his tail wagging.

'Terry Payne . . .'

He runs his finger down the list then frowns.

'You're at Autumn Lodge.'

He flicks through the attached sheets of paper.

'Yes, here we are. Autumn Lodge, along with Chloe Black-burn.'

I ignore the wolf whistles that accompany Chloe's name. Autumn Lodge? Funny name for a fitness club.

'Sir,' I ask, 'What's Autumn Lodge?'

Fitz is straight in with his two pennyworth.

'Don't you get it? You're working in an old people's home.'

I give Six Guns a pained glare.

'That's about the size of it, Terry.'

'But I wanted a gym.'

'No problem,' chuckles Fitz. 'You'll get fit lifting the old biddies.'

He puts on his best old woman's voice.

'Change my bedpan, sonny?'

I stare at Bobby in disbelief.

'And you thought you drew the short straw.'

Six Guns continues down his list, finally reaching Fitz's name.

'Here's somebody else who's got his first choice,' he says.

I grip the edge of the desk. No, it's not possible.

'You're assigned to the pony sanctuary in Hale. You're with

another of our pupils, Julie Carter. Maybe you can fix up joint transport, John. It's quite a trek.'

Fitz looks like the cat that got the cream. He's positively beaming.

'Are you all right?' Bobby asks me.

'Sure,' I tell him. 'For somebody who's just had their heart kicked out of their chest.'

Monday 26th June
12 noon

It's destiny. It's got to be. I'm at the front of the queue in the canteen and guess who arrives immediately after me?

That's right, Julie.

And that's not all. She's on her own. It's as though fate has drawn us together.

'No Kelly today?'

'Fifteen minute detention. She left her coursework at home.'

We're both smiling, big, shiny grins like we're telling the whole world how glad we are to see each other.

'Are you going to the end of year disco?' she asks.

OK, so how do I answer this one? If she's only making small talk I'd be mad to ask her to go with me. But what if she wants me to ask her and I don't? I mean, that's worse, isn't it? It's rejection. Oh God, why don't they do an instruction manual for this stuff. An A–Z of getting the girl. It would sell millions. I see Bobby come in behind Julie but he gives me the nod and goes off to sit by Caitlin. He's willing me to do the business. So what's holding me back? It's not like there's a force-field round her.

'Might do,' I say, playing it as cool as I can with a heat rash climbing my back. 'Bobby's band is playing. I've got to show my support. It's not my scene usually.'

I plump for chips and gravy followed by apple pie and custard. Julie goes for green salad and crusty bread with a pear to follow. The girl is a dietary saint.

'What about you?'

'I suppose I'll tag along with Kelly.'

She sounds disappointed. She does want me to ask her, I know it.

'Don't let on I've told you,' Julie says, leaning forward to confide in me, 'But she fancies Gary Tudor rotten.'

So that's why they were at footy practice. It wasn't to watch me, which I kind of knew already.

But it wasn't to watch Fitz either, which is brilliant. I smell Julie's hair and I feel giddy.

'My lips are sealed,' I tell her.

We hover awkwardly. Do I follow her to a table and sit next to her? It feels as if she willing me to do just that. But will I have enough to talk about if I do? I'm in an agony of indecision when Kelly arrives to make my mind up for me.

'Julie, Ju-lee! Over here, I've got something to tell you. Something amazing.'

Julie gives me a parting smile.

'Better see what she wants,' she says.

Is that a hint of regret in her voice? I'll never know. With a sinking heart I watch her go. Feeling suddenly very silly and very alone, I head for Bobby. He's my refuge in the storm.

'Well,' he says. 'Tell all, maestro.'

I glance at Caitlin. I feel uncomfortable talking with her around.

'There's nothing to tell.'

'Oh, you didn't let her slip through your fingers again!'

'Behave, will you. She wasn't in my fingers in the first place.'

If only, if only . . .

'Terry, Terry, Terry,' says Bobby. 'What will I do with you?'

'Leave it, eh?'

I chance a furtive glance in Julie's direction. She's in deep conversation with Kelly when Fitz arrives and makes a beeline straight for them. Kelly nudges Julie and the two of them greet Fitz with broad smiles. He's got everything on his side: the gym club connection, the Anfield connection, the beautiful people connection. And Fitz isn't hanging about, not like me.

'He's one lad who doesn't let the grass grow under his feet,' says Bobby.

I glare at Fitz. I wish it would grow all over his stupid face.

44

I'm on the bench for the Blackridge game. Everybody's nervous. It's the latest we've ever played, a month after the end of the football season proper. It's all to do with exams and stuff, and building work after a minor fire in our changing rooms a few weeks ago. As a result, this final has been postponed twice. Fitz and Gary Tudor are over the ball waiting for the whistle. Julie and Kelly are about twenty yards away, giggling excitedly about something.

Not me, that's for certain. They haven't looked in my direction once since they arrived. The conversation in the dinner queue is ancient history. It may as well never have happened. Why, oh why, didn't I make my move? Am I trying to throw her into Fitz's arms?

'Which team's Knowsley Manor?' asks Amy.

I've had to run all the way to her school to pick her up, then rush her back here. Mum doesn't knock off until five-thirty, so I'm stuck with her.

'Ssh.'

'But I don't know who to cheer for.'

'We're in the Inter Milan strip.'

'Which is that?'

Sisters!

'Black and blue stripes and black shorts. Don't you know anything?'

'I know more than you do!'

'Come on, Knowsley Manor,' screeches Amy.

'Knock it off, will you? You're embarrassing me.'

'No, I'm not.'

'Amy, I think I know if I'm embarrassed.'

'Terry, you don't even know when you're stupid.'

Fitz gets the game underway. Amy is immediately jumping up and down, making more noise than all the other spectators put together.

'Who's this?' Fitz asks as he takes a throw in front of us. 'Your girlfriend? Like them young, don't you?'

'She's my sister,' I hiss, gritting my teeth.

Fitz tears off down the line to get the return ball.

'He's good,' says Amy.

Too good.

At half-time we're 1–0 down, a defensive mix-up.

'You stay right here,' I tell Amy.

'Why, where are you going?'

'I've got to go to the team talk.'

'But you're not even playing.'

'I might be, in the second half.'

'Bet you're not.'

I decide not to grace her with a reply and join the rest of the team, mentally executing my little sister for crimes against humanity in general and me in particular. To my disappointment, there are no team changes after the break.

'Just keep pressing,' says Six Guns. 'We don't deserve to be behind. Retain possession as we're doing and we'll get our chances.'

I search among the twenty or so spectators for Julie. She's standing alone, brushing her hair. Kelly's watching Gary Tudor. I watch Julie snap a purple bobble round the thick, glossy mane and long to run my hands over it.

'It's never going to happen,' comes a voice.

I turn. It's Kelly.

'I've seen you staring at Julie,' she says. 'Can't take your eyes off her. You don't think she'd go out with a Manc, do you? You've got no chance.'

It makes sense. Julie's the new girl, but in the gym club crowd she had a ready-made social scene. Plus they all support Liverpool. It was obvious she'd hang around with them. After all, I'm just a ginger Manc. I feel a rush of temper.

'That so?' I retort. 'Well, you've got no chance with Gary Tudor either.'

Kelly blushes to the roots of her California-blonde hair.

'Who told you I fancy Gary?'

Panic sweeps through me like a long and very violent shiver. What have I done? Julie told me in confidence and I've blurted it right out.

'Nobody. Look, I didn't mean . . .'

46

'You're stupid, you know that? And nasty. Don't you come near me, or Julie.'

I watch her stamp away and I want the ground to swallow me up. I see them talking. After a few moments Julie turns her head and glares at me. Her eyes are cold. She knows I've betrayed her.

I'm a ginger Manc all right; a *suicidal* ginger Manc.

I'm sorry, Julie.

Sorry, sorry, sorry.

I feel like I've broken a precious vase and I know I'll never be able to stick it together again, no matter how hard I try.

Sorry.

Monday 26th June
5.15 p.m.

'I'm hungry.'

Amy has started the moment we get home.

'Just give me a minute, will you?' I snap. 'Let me get through the door.'

'What's the matter with you?' asks Amy. 'You'd think you'd lost.'

In fact, we won 3–1. Gary and Paul got the first two and Fitz scored the third to put the game beyond Blackridge. It was a sickener watching him parade round the field holding up the trophy. It was even worse watching Julie jumping up and down, eyes sparkling, clapping fit to burst.

'And I don't want a butty,' says Amy. 'I had butties for dinner.'

'I'll do you chicken nuggets and micro-chips,' I tell her. 'Just give me a minute.'

I march into the kitchen stamping on Fitz's face with every step I take. I stab four Frisky Fitzy chicken nuggets and put them under the grill. Finally, I put a packet of chips in the microwave, wishing Fitz was shrunk to six inches and trapped inside.

I imagine the explosion as his guts and brains dribble down the inside of the microwave and his eyes pop like corn, but when the beeper tells me the chips are done, fat, steaming chips is all I see. No microwaved bits of John Fitzpatrick glistening on the glass plate.

'Here's your tea,' I shout.

'Aren't you having anything?' Amy asks.

'No,' I tell her. 'I don't feel like it.'

The truth is I feel sick.

Sick to the pit of my stomach.

6

'Keys,' says Mum. 'Has anybody seen my car keys?'

'On top of the freezer,' I tell her.

'The freezer,' she says. 'What were they doing there?'

'You put them down when you were sneaking that Crunchie ice cream.'

Mum glares at me, before prodding a finger at the corners of her mouth looking for chocolate crumbs. She obviously thinks nobody has noticed her secret nibbles. I think the theory goes something like this: *If nobody sees me eat it, it's got no calories.*

'Amy,' she calls, 'Are you ready?'

I hear Amy come thumping downstairs in her riding boots.

'See you, Terry,' pants Mum. 'We'll be back about eight.'

'OK.'

'And if you go out, put the alarm on.'

'Got it.'

I hear a sharp intake of breath.

'Are you listening to me, Terry?'

'Sure. Back at eight, put on alarm. I heard every word.'

'See you then.'

'Yes, see you Mum. See you, Amy.'

Amy ignores me. She usually does these days. She doesn't like me picking her up from school. In fact, I'd go so far as to say she hates it. Can't say I'm wild about it, myself. I glance at the kitchen clock. Bobby said he'd be round about five. He's late. I can't wait to see him. It's been a long while.

What with work experience, I've hardly seen anybody and I'm desperate for news about Julie. Bobby gets to know

49

everything through the grapevine. Julie tells Kelly. Kelly tells Pepsey. Pepsey tells Caitlin and Caitlin tells Bobby. I remember what Caitlin said in the canteen: *Fitz is like an octopus*. I just hope he hasn't got his tentacles on Julie yet. I'm smashing a Frisky Fitzy lump of potato with my fork when the doorbell rings. There's Bobby on the doorstep with a grin as wide as the Grand Canyon.

'Hi Terry, how's it hanging?'

'Come in,' I grunt moodily.

'Whew, somebody's in a good mood. Hey, new haircut.'

'Yes, I got it done yesterday.'

I'm feeling really self-conscious about it. I still remember saying the words I thought I would never utter:

I want it like Michael Owen.

'Did you know that in your lifetime you will grow nine hundred and fifty kilometres of hair? What's it supposed to be anyway? Paul Scholes?'

Part of me is disappointed that Bobby doesn't recognise the style. Another part is relieved that my intentions aren't too transparent.

'It isn't supposed to be anybody,' I tell him. 'Just so long as I don't look like Chris Evans. Anyway, stop wittering and tell me what you know about Julie.'

Bobby perches on the arm of the couch and sips slowly from a can of Seven-Up. He's only doing it to build the suspense.

'You've blown it good style,' he tells me. 'That stuff about Gary Tudor. A definite own goal there, my son.'

'Yes, I know all that. But what about her and Fitz?'

'Which do you want first: the good news or the bad news?'

'Good news.'

'They're not going out yet.'

My heart gives a little skip for joy, though I don't like the way he added the word *yet* . . .

'And the bad news?'

'They're both working an extra day this Saturday. There's an open day at the Sanctuary.'

'You mean they're working an extra day when they don't have to? For free?'

Bobby nods.

'Be suspicious. Be very suspicious.'

'Fitz is about the most selfish person I know,' I say.

Actually, I don't really know what he's like, but I don't care. I hate him.

'He doesn't volunteer for things.'

'He does now.'

Bobby crushes the empty can and tosses it in the litter basket.

'So how're things?'

'Here? Pretty much the same. Dad's got himself a flat. Mum's on a diet, but she's stuffing herself on the quiet. I think she's missing him.'

'Tell her to get a new man. You burn 6.4 calories a minute through passionate kissing.'

He realises I don't want to think about Mum passionately kissing anybody and changes the subject.

'How was Wrinkly Dell?'

'It's called Autumn Lodge.'

'Whatever. How did it go?'

'It was all right, funnily enough. There was hardly any slobbering. I was working with Chloe Blackburn. We were a good team.'

Bobby winks suggestively but I ignore him.

'We got a really good report from the manager. Mum was dead pleased. How did your work experience go?'

'I was in the sports department.'

'What was that like?'

'Boring, but there were some nice perks.'

'Perks?'

'One perk actually. There was this girl from the south end.'

'Girl?'

'Rosie Ogunbiyi. She was on work experience too. I've already burned up about 120 calories on her.'

He's showing off. I bet it's more like 12.8 calories, then something else occurs to me.

'What about Caitlin?'

'What about her?'

'Have you two finished?'

'Course not.'

51

'So . . . ?'

'So I'm dating two girls at once. Big deal. It's not like we're married or anything.'

Suddenly I'm seeing Bobby in a completely different light. Good grief, the boy's a love-cheat!

'Bobby, that's rotten.'

'Behave yourself, what's rotten about it?'

'It's not fair on either of them.'

'Terry, it's a bit of fun. I'm fifteen, for crying out loud. Everybody does it at our age.'

'I don't,' I exclaim indignantly.

'Well, that's for sure. Terry, you don't even have *one* girl-friend.'

'Got to rub it in, haven't you?'

'Sorry, but I don't see what right you've got to judge me. I'm only doing what comes naturally.'

After a few moments of simmering silence I give him a playful punch on the arm.

'You're right. Take no notice. I'm all wound up over Julie.'

'You've only yourself to blame for that, Terry lad.'

Ain't that the truth!

Friday 7th July
8.00 p.m.

I see the car pull up and open the door for Mum and Amy.

'Was that Bobby I saw at the top of the road?' Mum asks.

'Yes, he came round to bring me up to date with all the goss.'

'He's going home early, isn't he?'

I close the door behind them.

'He isn't going home. He says he got a hot date.'

'With Caitlin?'

I hesitate, trying to picture Rosie Ogunbiyi. Bobby didn't say which one he was going out with.

'Yeah, of course with Caitlin.'

'So you're staying in?'

I nod.

'I don't want to play gooseberry to those two. Besides, they're going to see Mission Impossible 2. I saw it last week.'

'Did you? Who with?'

It was an Access Alley event, courtesy of Dad. A movie, then back to his new flat with a KFC. The flat isn't much to write home about, a pokey two-bedroomed affair above a video shop. I wonder what was so awful about living here to drive him to Grotland.

'Dad took Amy in to see Stuart Little and paid for me to go to MI-2.'

'That was good of him.'

She delivers the line heavy on the sarcasm.

'Have you two had an argument?' I ask her.

'Fat chance of that,' says Mum. 'We've hardly spoken for a fortnight. Mr Monosyllable, that's your dad. Oh, by the way, he wants you to phone him. It's about tomorrow.'

I'm about to give him a call when I notice a leaflet on the table.

'What's this?' I ask.

'Give that here!' shouts Amy. 'That's mine.'

'Hang on, I only want to read it.'

'Mu-um, Terry's robbed my leaflet.'

'Give it to her, Terry. I was going to take Amy tomorrow.'

'I haven't robbed it,' I tell Mum. 'I'm curious, that's all.'

'You?' says Mum. 'Since when were you interested in horses?'

Since Julie started work experience at the pony sanctuary, that's since when. I skim the details:

OPEN DAY

Horse and Pony Sanctuary
Lane Ends Farm,
Hale village.

Domestic and rare breeds,
pony rides, bouncy castle,
and much, much more.

It's the one Julie's at, all right.

'Tell you what, Mum,' I say, 'you have the day off. I'll ask Dad to take both of us.'

Mum does a double-take.

'You? With Amy to a pony sanctuary?'

'Yes. Why, what's up?'

Mum and Amy are staring at me open-mouthed like a couple of goldfish. As I pick up the phone I'm not altogether sure whether this is a good idea. It seems too much like snooping. But there's no going back now. It's something I've got to do.

Saturday 8th July
11.00 a.m.

'I hope you know who you look like with that haircut?' says Dad disgustedly as we walk down the path to the pony sanctuary. In his eyes, Michael Owen is Public Enemy No. 1 ever since an over-the-top tackle on Ronny Johnsen.

Amy stares at me.

'Who?'

'Only that little diver Owen.'

I can feel my face burning. It's as though I've betrayed the Red Devils.

'Don't be daft. I just wanted it short, that's all.'

'Mm.'

Dad's giving me suspicious looks all the way to the farm. Before you know it he'll be bringing me up on a charge of going soft on Liverpool.

Are you now, or have you ever been, sympathetic to Liverpool Football Club?

Maybe I'll plead the Fifth Amendment and decline to answer on the grounds that it might incriminate me.

Dad pays the admission and we go in. My stomach is churning, but there's no sign of Julie.

'Oh, isn't he beautiful!' cries Amy, heading straight for a Shetland pony.

'Just looks like a sawn-off horse to me,' I grunt.

'What's the matter with you?' asks Dad. 'This *was* your idea.'

I shrug my shoulders.

'Is it OK if I wander round by myself?'

'I don't see why not.'

I roam aimlessly around the stables and the various rides and stalls. There is no sign of Julie, though I bump into Dad and Amy twice. It's hard to avoid them at such a small event. At least Amy's having a good time. By the time I bump into them the second time, she's had a donkey ride and helped to groom a big Shire horse. Eventually I find myself at the far end of the grounds by a Dutch barn. I see Amy on the bouncy castle and give her a wave. She actually waves back. This treat has earned me a few brownie points.

'Are you lost, mate?' asks a man in his early twenties.

I'm obviously somewhere I shouldn't be.

'No, just looking round.'

That's when I hear a squeal – Julie's squeal. I turn round in time to see her come tumbling down the hay bales in the barn. She looks flushed and dishevelled. To my horror, Fitz comes tumbling after her. They're both covered in straw. So what did I expect? I've given the best-looking lad in school a free run and I wonder why he's taken advantage! Dufus Moronicus, that's me.

'Well, look who it isn't,' says Fitz, picking himself up and brushing himself down. 'And what have you done to your hair? Look at the state of him, Julie. He's always copying me.'

Copying you? Not exactly. We're both copying Michael Owen. Julie stares at me, her expression a mixture of suspicion and surprise.

'Are you spying on us, Payne?' asks Fitz. 'Because if you are, I think that's pretty weird. Don't you think he's weird, Julie?'

Julie is still picking the straw from her hair. She looks completely embarrassed by my arrival.

'What are you doing here, Terry?'

I wish I could just beam up and be a zillion miles away. This was a really bad idea. What on earth did I expect to achieve?

'I saw a leaflet, that's all. My little sister's really into horses.'

As I speak, my legs are turning to jelly.

'Pull the other one,' says Fitz. 'You're a stalker, that's what you are.'

He's really enjoying my discomfort. He knows I've built another obstacle between myself and Julie.

'Imagine that, Ju, you've got your very own stalker.'

I wince at the familiar *Ju*.

'I am not a stalker,' I retort. 'I didn't even know this was the farm you were working at.'

Which is when things go from bad to worse.

'Yes he did,' comes a familiar voice behind me.

My heart sinks. It's Kelly. The girl is glued to Julie. What is she, her personal bodyguard?

She's wearing a Chicago Bulls baseball cap that makes her look more like Sabrina than ever.

'He's had Bobby Quinn pumping my friends for info about you, Julie. You don't want anything to do with him. He'll be rummaging in your bin next. Weirdo.'

I look around in panic. My scalp is prickling under this traitor's haircut and Kelly's jibes have penetrated right to the quick. The day has turned into a complete disaster. I want out.

'It's not true,' I stutter. 'I only . . .'

Compared to Fitz and Kelly, Julie is almost sympathetic. She speaks to me in a gentle, level way, more in regret than anger. But that doesn't make her next words any easier to take:

'Terry, why don't you just go?'

Saturday 8th July
1 p.m.

I'm going, all right, but only after I've endured Amy trying every single activity going. It's been awful. My flesh is creeping right off my bones. Fitz is really enjoying my embarrassment, of course. He keeps turning up, running his hand over his haircut, making out I'm trying to look just like him. Oh great, there he is again.

'Going so soon, Terry? And just when the fun was starting.'

He jerks his head in the direction of Julie. She's giving the little kids rides on one of the Shetland ponies. She's so nice, so perfect for me I could cry. I really hate Fitz.

'Do you know that lad, Terry?' asks Dad as he closes the farm gate behind us.

'He's at our school. He's here on work experience.'

I don't mention Julie. I think if I tried to say her name I'd give the game away. It's hard trying to sound cheerful when

you've got stinging eyes and a lump in your throat, but I
manage to sound composed. At least, I think I do.

'Did you have a good time then?' asks Dad.

'Oh Dad, it was lovely.'

Amy looks at me with shining eyes.

'Thanks Terry.'

At least I've got one girl on my side. Unfortunately, it isn't
the one I want.

'Any time, Amy. World's greatest big brother, that's me.'

We get in the car and I give the pony sanctuary a last look.
There's no sign of Julie and Fitz. Good job. I probably wouldn't
like what I saw. Looks like I've left the way wide open for him.
As we hit the M57 Dad puts a tape on. The first song is 'Is she
really going out with him?' by Joe Jackson.

Amy immediately wants the radio on instead. Joe Jackson
gives way to 'Reach for the stars' by S Club 7. Thank goodness
for little sisters.

7

It's the end of term. It's just crept up on me. The last twelve days have gone by in a haze. After the pony sanctuary fiasco I've been too gutted to notice the passing days.

'You're not doing it, Bobby. There's no way I'm turning up tonight if you do that.'

I'm talking about Bobby's little Alison speech. He still thinks his corny song dedication can salvage something with Julie. He's actually been planning to put me on the spot in the middle of the school disco. It's a good job I've rumbled his little plot.

'You need something to sting you into action, Terry. A bomb up the bum, something like that.'

'Look, I'm not having you playing Cupid. Stop interfering, Bobby. I can sort myself out, thank you very much.'

He gives me a sideways look as if to say: *Can you really?*

'Oh, get a life Bobby.'

'I've got one,' he retorts smugly. 'Two, actually.'

There's a twinkle in his eye. He means Caitlin and Rosie, of course.

'Which one are you taking out tonight?'

'Oh Caitlin, of course. It's got to be Caitlin around school. What do you think I am, stupid?'

'So when are you seeing this Rosie?'

'Tomorrow night. We're going bowling near hers.'

'You're going to get a reputation the way you're going.'

Bobby grins more smugly than ever.

'Don't worry about me, Terry lad, I know what I'm doing.'

'Are you sure about that?'

'Positive. Now tell me, if you don't want my help, how are you going to rekindle the gorgeous Julie's love for you?'

'What do you mean rekindle?' I reply. 'There was no fire in the first place. Not from her anyway.'

'I'm not so certain.'

My whole insides turn over.

'Have you heard something?'

'Not really. It's just, when I've seen her with you, there seems to be a bit of a spark.'

I shake my head.

'You're imagining it.'

But what if he's not? A chance, imagine if there's a chance.

'Hey, take it from your uncle Bobby. I'm an expert in these things.'

'Well, this time you're barking up the wrong tree. You should have seen her face when I turned up at the pony sanctuary.'

Bobby shrugs.

'OK, so you dropped a brick there. You embarrassed her in front of everybody. But it was a tactical mistake, not a strategic defeat. It doesn't mean she doesn't like you.'

I'm dying to believe him. Sure, what's a tactical mistake between friends?'

'Honest,' Bobby says. 'She'll have got over it by now.'

'Says you. Bobby, not everybody bounces back the way you do.'

'Are you saying I'm fickle?'

'Well, you have got two girlfriends on the go at the same time.'

'Terry, I'm hurt.'

He says it in a way that makes it obvious he isn't. He's loving every moment of it.

'So you don't want my help tonight?'

'Don't you dare.'

'Fine, it's your look-out.'

'Exactly,' I say. 'It's my look-out. Anyway, I've got to go. I'll be late for our Amy.'

As I turn away, Fitz walks past. Just as he's done every time he's seen me for the last week and a half, he pats his hair and winks at me, all superior. I really hate that lad. And to think, once upon a time I wanted to be him.

'Be at the school hall for half past six,' Bobby shouts after me. 'You can help us set up.'

'OK,' I answer. 'So long as you don't try to set me up. Oh, by the way. I'll have a surprise for you.'

'What's that?'

I glance in Fitz's direction.

'It won't be a surprise if I tell you.'

Thursday 20th July
3.45 p.m.

'But I'm hungry,' protests Amy.

'Look, I'll do the tea the moment we get in. Come on, it'll only take fifteen minutes.'

Amy looks doubtfully at the barber's.

'Look, I'll get you something from the newsagents. I'll pay for it out of my own money.'

'Like what?'

'You name it. Any sweet you want.'

I see the look in her face. She's wondering how much she can squeeze out of me.

'OK,' I say. 'Look, I'll go up to 60p. You can pick two things, one for now and one for after your tea. I won't even let on to Mum. Deal?'

Amy is thinking mega-sugar boost. Right now, she'll go along with just about anything.

'Deal.'

She nearly snatches my hand off.

'OK,' I say. 'You go to the newsagents and meet me back here. I want to get inside quick while there's no queue.'

By the time Amy returns, most of Michael Owen lies on the floor of the barber's. I see the look of horror on her face. Two minutes later the deed is done and I pay the barber.

'Mum will kill you,' says Amy the moment we're outside. 'You're bald.'

'I am not bald,' I say, viewing myself self-consciously in the chemist's window. 'It's only a number two.'

'Mum will still kill you,' says Amy.

'Don't be silly,' I tell her. 'She won't mind.'

Thursday 20th July
5.45 p.m.

'Oh my God!' cries Mum. 'You look like a convict.'

'It's only a number three,' I say.

'You said it was a number two,' says Amy, interrupting.

'I lied.'

'You're a skinhead. My son's a skinhead. Why didn't you ask me to cut it?'

'Because you wouldn't have cut it short enough,' I tell her.

'What was wrong with the way you had it?' Mum asks.

'I looked like Michael Owen,' I explain.

'So? He's a good-looking boy. Not a thug either, not like that Roy Keane.'

'Mum, Michael Owen's the enemy. He plays for Liverpool.'

'Oh, but why quite so short? You look like an urchin out of Oliver Twist.'

Honestly, first a convict, then a skinhead, now an urchin. Mum, you do wonders for my self-esteem.

'I felt like a change.'

That's not the real reason, of course. If the Michael Owen had done the trick with Julie, I don't think I'd have ever changed it.

Real reason number 1: it'll get Fitz off my back.

Real reason number 2: I won't feel like a traitor.

Real reason number 3: it's so short you can hardly tell I'm ginger. Now nobody will mistake me for Chris Evans.

'Are you going to the school disco like that?' asks Mum.

'No,' I say sarcastically, 'I'm wearing a blond wig. Of course I'm going like this.'

'Well, put some nice clothes on.'

'Mum, I'm quite capable of choosing my own clothes.'

'I just hope you do better with them than you have with your hair.'

Thursday 20th July
6.15 p.m.

I leave the house in a white T-shirt, sand chinos and oxblood loafers. It's in keeping with Bobby's mod obsession. Mum thinks I look smart – except for the hair. I catch my reflection in the chemist's again. OK, so it is a bit severe, emphasising my narrow face and prominent cheekbones, but at least Michael Owen is dead and buried. I smile with satisfaction at the thought of him being tossed in a black bin-bag and put out for the dustmen.

When I arrive at school *The Sons of Moe Szyszlak* are all but set up. Bobby's discussing input and output leads with the DJ while Caitlin sits dangling a pink shoe from the end of her toe.

I feel uncomfortable talking to her, knowing what I do about Bobby's other woman, but I make the effort.

'You look nice,' I say.

'Got to make the effort, haven't you,' she says, her eyes fixed on the top of my shorn head.

'I thought it would help me stay cool in the hot weather,' I say feebly.

'Mm,' says Caitlin unhelpfully. 'I preferred it the way it was.'

'Whoa!' cries Bobby, detaching himself from the DJ. 'If it isn't Fabien Barthez. So this is your surprise.'

I smile at the mention of the United keeper.

'It's not that extreme,' I say. 'Barthez is completely bald.'

Bobby grabs me and plants a kiss on my skull, just the way Laurent Blanc did to Barthez at Euro 2000.

'Let's see if Julie likes the hard man look.'

'Bobby,' I say. 'Do you really think an ectomorph can be hard?'

'Certainly,' he replies. 'As sure as I'm sitting here on this unicycle.'

I pull a face.

'Anyway,' he says, 'If you're not doing anything you can give me a hand with the speakers.'

Did I say I hate Fitz?

Well scrub that, I loathe him, abhor him, abominate him. You want to know why? Because he's everything I want to be.

He turned up about an hour ago in white casual trousers and what looks like a red gym vest, just so he could show off his arms. He's all biceps and triceps and all sorts of other ceps I don't know the name of. His arms are like a bag of grapefruit, all macho and bulging.

I detest him.

And it isn't just what he looks like, it's the way he's acting. He's been on the dancefloor for an hour. He knows every move to every song. S Club 7, Five, Alice Deejay, Steps, he can move to them all. You'd think he'd come across all nerdy and embarrassing, dancing with the girls like that. But he doesn't. He's the leader of the gang. Everybody's crowding round him, copying him. And just look at Julie. I mean, look at her! She's laughing and giggling at everything he does. He slides behind her during that corny *Grease* compilation, running his hands up and down her arms.

You're the one that I want.

He's the one that I hate.

He's everything I'd like to be: school football captain, top set in everything, boy band good looks. Julie was bound to give in eventually. After a few minutes, Julie detaches herself from the Frisky Fitzy Appreciation Society and goes for a drink. Accidentally on purpose, I find myself next to her in the queue. I can't take my eyes off her. She's wearing the little black dress. Simple but effective; so effective I find it hard to breathe as I follow her to the hatch where they're selling cans.

'Julie, I just wanted to say sorry about the pony sanctuary.'

She smiles, not the full Colgate treatment, more diplomatic and reserved than that.

'Forget it. I have.'

'I didn't want you thinking I was, you know, weird.'

'Terry, I know you're not weird.'

Despite everything, I'm sure I can detect a little warmth in her voice. I hesitate. She says I'm not weird. Is that good or bad?

'Enjoying yourself?'

'Oh yes, Fitz is a real laugh, isn't he?'

Sure, just a little bundle of joy, our Fitzy.

'You ought to let yourself go, you know. I've seen you hanging round. I bet you haven't had a single dance.'

Ask me then, *please* ask me.

Then a little voice inside my head says: *Behave, it should be you asking her.* Little Voice is right; even now it isn't too late. Go on, Terry lad, ask her. But all I end up saying is:

'I feel stupid.'

What a chat-up line that is: *Look at me, I'm stupid.*

We reach the hatch and Kelly and Pepsey come over. Kelly gives me a daggers look.

'Two more Diet Cokes,' says Julie. 'And a Tango for Fitz.'

The bottom drops out of my world. She's buying him drinks now.

'Love the hair,' says Kelly sarcastically. 'First Michael Owen, now David Beckham. You like to ring the changes, don't you.'

I know I've gone bright red. I watch helplessly as Kelly and Pepsey whisk Julie away. I catch Fitz's eye. He pats his head then roars with laughter. Suddenly I know how it feels to be two inches tall. I walk away from the hatch holding my Diet Coke and trying not to look gutted when the DJ's voice booms out of the speakers.

'Right, that's all from me for a few minutes. While I take a break, the music's going to be coming from a band drawn from Year 10 and 11 students at the school. Give it up for *The Sons of Moe Szyszlak.*'

The lights go off. Then a spotlight picks out a banner behind the band: Third Generation Mods. Then there are more lights and the four members of the group appear wearing Simpsons masks. There's Moe Szyszlak, Barney Gumble, Bart and Homer Simpson. After a round of applause and cheering, off come the masks.

Bobby counts the band in and they launch into 'Heatwave'. I watch Fitz skipping across the dancefloor. He even knows what to do to the Golden Oldies. All the way through 'Come back and take this hurt off me', 'Eton Rifles' and 'I fought the law and the law won' the dancefloor's bouncing even though most of the dancers have never heard any of the numbers before.

Then I hear the words that make my heart turn to ice.

'This one's for my best friend Terry. Here's hoping he finds his Alison.'

Loads of pairs of eyes pick me out. Oh Bobby, no, I begged you. I pleaded with you. I stand gobsmacked as everybody pairs up for this classic slowie. I want to get away from this place, but not until I see where Julie is. I scan the dancefloor. Where is she? Then I see her. She's got her arms round Fitz's neck and her cheek's touching his. I want to scream.

Now I know what it feels like to be one inch tall. Somebody save me.

'Terry?'

I look round. It's Chloe Blackburn. She's wearing black trousers and a shiny white top. Even the way I'm feeling I can't help noticing she looks nice.

'Yes?'

'Look, I don't know who your Alison is, but I don't see you dancing with anyone.'

She's the one. Chloe's come to save me. She takes my hand and leads me onto the dancefloor. I follow her in a daze as the music wraps itself round me. I'm inside this cocoon of music and lights and the smell of Chloe's auburn hair. A girl has finally asked me to dance, but I hardly feel a thing. This isn't the girl I want to be with.

'Come closer.'

I do as I'm told. My hands are on Chloe's hips. She feels good pressed against me like this, but she's not Julie. I steal a glance to my left. There they are, swaying gently, Julie and Fitz. It's her eyes I catch first.

This is wrong, my eyes are telling her and, just for a moment, I feel she's saying the same thing back. Then it's Fitz looking back. He grins, wide and mocking, and squeezes Julie even tighter. Then I'm drowning, sinking in despair and music and the smell of Chloe's hair. So I cling to her . . .

. . . and she clings back.

PART TWO

Between Two Girls
or
Red Shirt, Red Face,
Red Mist

1

Girls are like buses. You wait forever for one, then two come along at once.

'So what are you going to do?' asks Bobby, stealing a glance at Dad. Dad's chatting to a fisherman just along the bank. He's just arrived to pick us up from overnight fishing. Well, you can do that sort of thing when you're in the middle of your six-week summer break. In fact, it's about the only time you can do it. School is no respecter of freedom. Dad has news. Mum's given him Chloe Blackburn's phone number to pass on to me. At least hostilities could be suspended long enough for her to do that. Seems Chloe's just got back off holiday and she wants me to give her a call.

Gulp!

I'm staring at the phone number wondering how to answer Bobby.

'Chloe's a nice girl,' says Bobby, packing his olive-green bivouac. 'You could do worse.'

'You sound like my mum,' I tell him as I empty the last of the unused bait into the lake.

My emotions are wriggling more feverishly than those maggots. My head's in a spin. I stare at the piece of paper Dad's just handed me. Chloe's number is written on it in red biro. The colour makes it seem urgent: phone me! Yes, you with the ginger stubble on your head: PHONE ME! I haven't seen either Julie or Chloe since we broke up from school for the summer. Julie vanished to Huyton, probably with Fitz in hot pursuit, and Chloe went off on holiday to Portugal with

69

her parents. For a fortnight life has been uncomplicated. Sure, I've thought about little else but Julie and Fitz and Chloe, but I haven't had to face them in the flesh. I've managed to put my heartache on the back-burner.

'You know what they say,' Bobby chips in unhelpfully. 'A bird in the hand's worth two in the bush.'

'What's that supposed to mean?' I demand irritably, packing my rod.

'Think about it,' says Bobby. 'You've had it with Julie, that's pretty obvious. She and Fitz are definitely an item. Time to forget her and get back out there in the field.'

Out there in the field! Bobby makes it sound like a game. Some game! I close my eyes. I can still see them at the disco, Julie with her head on Fitz's mesomorphic shoulder, him with his hands round her gym-conditioned waist. Just thinking about them, I feel like I'm boiling inside.

'It'll have to wait till home,' I say. 'I left my mobile on charge.'

'Here,' says Bobby, tossing me his. 'No time like the present. Give Chloe a call.'

Then Dad detaches himself from the angler and comes over.

'Hurry up and pack your stuff, lads. I want to get off home.'

Bobby starts to take his rod apart.

'I'll get a couple of choccie bars for the drive home while you're finishing off,' says Dad.

'Did you know that you will eat one hundred and sixty kilograms of chocolate in your life?' asks Bobby.

'No,' says Dad. 'I didn't, but I do now.'

He sets off the shop and I stare at the mobile. Bobby's mum insisted we brought it with us. She wasn't too happy about us spending the night at the lake. Neither was my mum. But Dad won them round, reminding them that we are nearly sixteen, and a spot of overnight fishing is a lot better than hanging round the streets. I expected Mum to start arguing with him, but she didn't. Not that it's a good sign. They've barely talked since Dad left at the end of June.

'Oh, come on Terry,' says Bobby, jabbing a finger at the phone number. 'The girl phoned you the moment she got back off holiday. She's crazy about you. You'd be a mug to pass up the chance.'

'Yes, but . . .'

'But what? She's a girl, not a bad-looking one, and she likes you. She's made the first move, for crying out loud! The first *two* moves, in fact.'

I think about the way she approached me at the disco. I think about the way she pushed up against me, so close I could hardly breathe. I think about her auburn hair and the way it smelled. I run my eyes over the phone number. Bobby's right, I could do worse.

'Go on, what's holding you back?'

'Not everybody's the same as you, Bobby. We can't all turn our feelings on and off like a lightswitch. I still care about Julie.'

Bobby ignores the dig about Caitlin and Rosie.

'Yes, and she cares about Frisky Fitzy, you wussie. Face it lad, you've been dumped good style. Trust me, it's better to be a dumper than a dumpee. Don't be such a mug.'

He's right. I'm sure he is. I *know* he is. Chloe and I kind of match. Like me, she's on the skinny side, freckle-faced and red-haired. Not too tall, either. I wouldn't be worried about looking like a dwarf the way I do next to Julie. Chloe's like me in her ways too. She's quite shy, though not too shy to ask me to dance. What the heck, Julie's gone. What have I got to lose?

'Well?'

'OK, I'll do it,' I tell him. 'I'm going over there so I can have a bit of privacy. No eavesdropping.'

Bobby holds up his hands and comes over all innocent.

'Me, listen in on a mate's private telephone call? As if I would.'

I give him a knowing look.

'Just stay put, right there.'

Bobby does his obedient dog impression and I can't help but smile. I see Dad making his way back from the fishery shop and hurry away to a secluded spot overlooked by some weeping willows. I punch in Chloe's number and take a deep breath.

'Hello?'

It's Chloe. Thank goodness it isn't her mum or dad.

'Hi Chloe, it's Terry.'

'Terry!'

She sounds so glad to hear my voice it makes my skin prickle. I shouldn't be doing this, not the way I still feel about Julie.

'I got a message to call you.'

'Yes, I've been thinking about you. You know, since the disco.'

'But how did you get my number?'

She giggles. I do too, not quite sure what I'm laughing about.

'Ever heard of the phone book?'

I remember how we stopped by NatWest Bank on the way home. Caitlin and Bobby were a few yards away, snogging the faces off each other. Chloe looked up at me expectantly and I kissed her. It felt really good, but all the while I was thinking of Julie.

'I thought maybe you wanted to see me again.'

This is it, Terry lad. Remember what Bobby always says: *Just do it.*

'Yes, I'd like that.'

There, done it. I'm amazed at myself. Chuffed to bits, really. Before I know it, we're talking excitedly about where we're going on our first date (her words, not mine). We make plans to go to Southport on Saturday.

I'm standing there for a couple of minutes after she hangs up, with a stupid grin all over my face. I've got a girlfriend! My first proper girlfriend. One who is keen enough to do all the chasing.

Then the bushes behind me shake.

'Bobby, you promised!'

But it isn't Bobby. It's the fisherman Dad was talking to, an old guy in his sixties. He's smiling at me.

'Young love, eh?' he says.

I know I must have gone bright red.

Yes, young love.

We dropped Bobby off on the way back, so here we are sitting in Dad's flat among the coffee cups and the Chinese take-away wrappers. The *Mirror* is open at the football section *Mania*. I read a line highlighted at the top of the page:

mania: noun, mental derangement marked by great excitement and (freq.) craze: passion (for).

Mental derangement marked by great excitement. That's me and Man U. all right. Me and Julie too, come to think of it. You can cut that out, I tell myself. You're with Chloe Blackburn now, so start acting like it. OK, so there's no mental derangement with Chloe. Big deal, I like her. She's pretty and nice and mad about me. That's enough, isn't it?

'What're you looking at?'

Dad glances at the headline over my shoulder. There's a picture of Liverpool's five summer signings and they're saying: *We're coming to get you Fergie!*

I already have the Day of Judgement in my head. December 16th. United v. Liverpool at Old Trafford.

'Wishful thinking,' says Dad. 'It's our title again. The bookies have got us odds on.'

'I hope you're right,' I say. 'I just wish we'd signed five new players. I can't believe we haven't got a single new outfield player. I mean, our defence leaked forty-three goals last season, more than any other title contender.'

'I know what you mean,' says Dad. 'That's why we got knocked out of the Champions' League. But just watch us in the Charity Shield. We'll batter Chelsea this Sunday. Fergie knows what he's doing.'

Fergie might, but do I? As I look at Nick Barmby grinning at the camera, I see Julie's head superimposed on that Liverpool shirt. Come December 16th, one of us will be on cloud nine, the other in the dead zone. My skin prickles with Julie-fever. Mental derangement, you can say that again!

'So who's this Chloe then?' Dad asks.

'Just a girl.'

Dad nods knowingly.

'Ah, just a girl.'

'Yes, just a girl. Can we leave it at that?'

'Sure. What do you want to do this Saturday?'

Saturday! I do a double-take. First, because everything Bobby predicted about our Access days has come true. It hasn't taken Dad long to run out of ideas. Second, because I've already told Chloe I'd go to Southport with her.

'Sorry Dad,' I reply finally. 'I'm busy this Saturday.'

'Busy?' Dad asks, his face falling. 'Busy how?'

'Chloe,' I tell him. 'I said I'd go to Southport with her.'

'Ah.'

'You don't mind?'

'Course not. Nice to see that one of us is having some luck with his love life.'

I grimace to indicate I don't really want to know. Just because I hang around with him doesn't mean he's forgiven.

Dad nods.

'Looks like it's just me and Amy.'

'Sorry.'

'Don't be, son. You're growing up.'

'Anyway,' I say, feeling quite pleased with myself for finally having a girlfriend. 'I'd better be off.'

'Want a lift back?'

'No, it'll only take me ten minutes.'

I fold the *Mirror* and slide it into the magazine rack. That's where I find a copy of *Men's Health*. There's this bloke on the cover with biceps like Spanish onions and veins like pipe-cleaners.

'What's this doing here?' I ask, nodding at the old man's beer belly. My dad reading *Men's Health*? It makes about as much sense as Roy Keane with a knitting pattern.

'I've decided to get into shape,' says Dad.

A moment's hesitation then the confession: 'As a matter of fact, I've joined a gym.'

Now, just you hang on there, father of mine. Gym = membership fee = broken promises.

'You've what!'

There's horror in my voice. Anger too.

'What's the matter with that?'

'Do I need to spell it out?' I yell. 'You cancel our United season tickets, then you blow the money on some stupid gym.'

'Oh, now that's not fair,' Dad replies. 'It's nothing fancy, just a council fitness suite. It doesn't add up to a fraction of what it costs to go to Old Trafford.'

I shake my head. Right now, I don't want to hear balance sheets. Or reasoned argument. In short, I don't want to hear Dad. All I know is, he's traded in my treasured season ticket and now he's wasting the money trying to get fit.

All I get out of the arrangement is lousy Access days.

'So why do you want to get fit all of a sudden?' I ask. 'You've been happy being a slob all these years.'

I see a flicker of embarrassment in his face. I'm thinking aftershave and hair gel. I'm thinking new gear from Next.

'You're after some woman,' I gasp. 'You're going out on the pull, aren't you?'

I think of Mum secretly working her way through a packet of cookies and wondering what she's done wrong and all of a sudden I'm seeing Dad through slime-tinted spectacles.

Home-wrecker!

Season-ticket canceller!

And now – womaniser!

'Dad, you're a dirty old man.'

I slam the door and stamp down the stairs. Seeing him open his door to call after me I shout up at him:

'Dirty old man!'

Thursday 10th August
8.45 p.m.

'That you, Terry?' shouts Mum.

'Nah, Jack the Ripper.'

She appears at the living room door. I notice the telltale Hobnob crumbs nestling in the folds of her top.

'Is it too much to ask for a normal answer?' she asks, brushing away the evidence.

'Probably.'

I see a flash of temper in her eyes and backtrack quickly.

'Sorry. I'm spending too much time with Bobby. Where's Amy?'

'She's at Katie's. She's sleeping over.'

'Oh yeah, I forgot.'

'Did your dad give you that girl's phone number?'

At the mention of Dad my cheeks start to burn, but I manage not to let it show.

'Yes, I phoned her.'

'And?'

'And we're going to Southport on Saturday.'

Mum's wearing this sickly smile.

'So who is she?'

'A girl, Mum, female of the species. Her name's Chloe.'

'When do I get to meet her?'

I take a deep breath.

'Mum, it's our first date. No need to buy a new hat quite yet.'

She looks away and I realise it's probably not too good an idea to make wedding jokes.

'You OK?'

'Of course,' she says, 'Why do you ask?'

I point out the Hobnob crumbs.

'I've been at a bit of a loss tonight,' she admits. 'It felt so strange being in on my own.'

She bites her lower lip.

'You know I even got two cups out when I made myself a coffee.'

'Dad, you mean?'

Mum nods.

'I just can't get used to him not being around. I've been part of *us* so long I've forgotten how to be *me*. You know what I am, I'm the clockwork key in everybody's back. I wind you and Amy up and send you off to school. I used to wind your Dad up and send him off to work. When I got married, I thought it was for good. Marriage was what I did. I cooked, I cleaned, I made a home. Now I don't really know what I am.'

I listen in silence. God, she sounds down.

'Terry, can I ask you something?

'Fire away.'

76

'Has Geoff said anything? Has he ever told you why he left?'

I'm feeling uncomfortable. What does she think I am, a Relate counsellor?

'He did say one thing.'

Mum's looking at me all expectant.

'He said he didn't get the butterflies any more.'

She looks shocked. For a moment or two she doesn't say a thing. Then she looks annoyed. 'He said that! So that's why he's decided to walk away from seventeen years of marriage, is it? Butterflies! Well, believe you me, Geoffrey Payne, I haven't felt the butterflies for years, and *I* wasn't about to walk out.'

She stamps into the living room. I wander into the kitchen wishing I'd kept my mouth shut and return a couple of minutes later. There's only one thing for it. I hold out the biscuit barrel.

'Hobnob?'

2

'I don't believe this!'

'What happened to the marking? What was Johnsen doing leaving Hasselbaink clear?'

We're 1–0 down to Chelsea in the Charity Shield and it hurts. I hate Chelsea. I mean, I really hate them. They beat us 5–0 at Stamford Bridge last season and I wanted revenge today. It's not just the scoreline that bothers me. It's the way the two sides are playing. Chelsea have carved out three or four gilt-edged opportunities and we haven't even got off the blocks.

'Don't panic,' says Dad. 'Plenty of time to go. Keano will get them organised.'

But Keano doesn't even get himself organised. Hasselbaink treads on the United captain's ankle and Keano sees red. From then on it's only a matter of time before he goes into the ref's book. I see him moving up behind Gustavo Poyet and I hold my breath. The telltale signs are there. The red mist has descended.

'Don't do it,' I hiss, gripping the edge of the couch.

But he does it, does it with knobs on, hacking into the back of Poyet's left leg right in front of the referee. Yellow card, please let it be yellow. We don't want to go into the new season with Keano on a three-match suspension.

But it isn't yellow. It's red. Keano's off. I look at Dad. He shrugs.

'We lost the last two Charity Shields,' he reminds me. 'It didn't stop us winning the Premiership both times.'

Always look on the bright side of life, that's Dad's signature tune.

'Just think about it,' he says. 'Two years ago Arsenal beat us 3–0 in this fixture and we still won the Treble.'

Somehow it doesn't help. I'm watching my beloved Reds being taken to the cleaners by Vialli's bunch of international playboys and nothing can ease the agony. I imagine Julie and Fitz are sitting together on a couch somewhere right now lapping this up. Liverpool are playing a friendly against the Italian side, Parma. I just hope they're losing too.

'We might as well switch the TV off now,' I tell Dad.

'Give over,' he says. 'Have you forgotten when Keano got sent off against Arsenal in the FA Cup semi-final? We still won then.'

Always look on the bright side of life.

Dee doo, dee doo, dee doo, dee doo.

But it isn't going to happen this time. That evening, Ryan Giggs was on fire. This afternoon he's a damp squib. He looks like he's only come along to make up the numbers. With only one shot on target we look completely toothless. Things go from bad to worse when Melchiot slips the ball through Stam's legs. 2–0. When the final whistle goes, Dad and I bolt for the kitchen together. It's an unwritten law. We never watch the other side lift the trophy when we lose. Instead, we pretend it never happened.

'Toasted sausage sandwich?' asks Dad.

'Fine.'

'One or two?'

'One.'

When I'm gutted, I go all monosyllabic. It's better than crying. We switch the TV off and eat.

'So how did your date go?'

'It was good.'

The pain of defeat is easing. I'm up to three syllables already.

'What did you do?'

'You know, stuff.'

We did stuff all right. We went on the roller coasters, held hands, licked ice creams, drank Coke, ate fish and chips, kissed. We kissed straight after the fish and chips. Chloe's lips tasted of batter and vinegar. She could have tasted of petrol, I would still have enjoyed kissing her.

'Don't give much away, do you?'

I grin.

'Like father, like son.'

'Meaning?'

'Mum asked me if I knew why you'd walked out.'

'What did you tell her?'

'What you told me. That you didn't feel the butterflies any more.'

Dad rolls his eyes.

'I bet that went down well.'

'Not very. She was really annoyed.'

I look straight at him.

'So *is* that why you went? The butterflies, I mean?'

Dad sighs.

'Pretty much. Don't get me wrong. Your mother's great. I feel terrible walking out on her. Life was just so routine. Every day was the same. It felt like I was wading through treacle.'

'And that's it?'

'You don't understand, do you?'

That's an understatement. He breaks up a whole family because of a butterfly deficiency. I'm like Mum. I believe in one boy, one girl, happy ever after. Sad? Maybe, but that's the way I'm made.

'Look, do you get the butterflies with this Chloe?'

'Yes.'

It's true, I do. Little ones that creep up from the pit of my stomach until I've got a lump in my throat. But no matter how I try to tell myself otherwise, I know it's nothing to what I'd feel with Julie. With her, I'd have butterflies the size of vultures. Genetically-enhanced butterflies. Let's face it, I'm talking butterfly-mania!

'And it feels good, doesn't it?'

I remember the way we sat together on the platform at Southport station. Chloe rested her head on me and I felt like I'd won the lottery. I even forgot Julie for a while.

'Of course it does.'

'Then just imagine being with somebody for seventeen

years. You wake up one morning and you think: am I never going to feel that way again?'

I feel disloyal to Mum just listening to him. I know that she's in the right and he's in the wrong. But I want to hear more. I mean, this could be my future.

'Mum says the butterflies went for her too,' I tell him. 'She says there's more to marriage.'

Dad shakes his head.

'Maybe for her.'

He looks sadly at his half-eaten toastie.

'When you first fall for a woman, you feel so alive. I just wanted that thrill again.'

I listen to him, but I don't quite know what to make of it. I look round his pokey flat. He seems to have given up a lot, just for a thrill.

'Believe me, Terry,' he says, 'There could come a time when you're with somebody, and no matter how good it feels, you find yourself wanting more.'

I think of Chloe and how warm and comfortable everything feels with her. Then I think of Julie and I know I would give it up right here, right now, if she only gave me one iota of encouragement.

Dad, I know the feeling already.

Sunday 13th August
6.30 p.m.

I'm walking past Prescot station when I hear it. Fitz's voice.

'So what was the score today, Terry?'

I look in the direction of his crowing voice and my stomach turns over. Walking towards me are Julie and Fitz, Kelly and Gary Tudor. They're all kitted out in their Liverpool shirts. Gary, Kelly and Fitz are wearing the home strip. Julie's wearing black pedal-pushers and the new gold away shirt.

'You know the score,' I grunt.

'Go on,' says Fitz. 'Just for me, say the scoreline.'

He puts a hand behind his right ear.

'How did the mighty Man U. do today?'

Julie's watching me, wondering how I'll react. I need to stay cool.

'You know very well,' I tell him. 'We lost. 2–0.'

'Did Roy Keane have a good game?' asks Gary Tudor.

'Get stuffed!' I snap hotly.

So much for staying cool.

'No need to be like that,' says Kelly, Sabrina-cheeks dimpling under her Liverpool baseball cap. 'We were just wondering how the Footballer of the Year got on.'

I turn to go. The back of my neck is prickling. I've got this neon sign flashing away in my head. December 16th. Manchester United v. Liverpool. Suddenly it's situation critical. It's bad enough having four Liverpool fans on your back. But when one of them is Julie . . .

'You haven't asked how we got on,' says Fitz. 'We've just got back from Anfield.'

'You mean you went to the game?'

I glance from Fitz to Julie. I can just see them hugging as the goals go in. Please let it be a Parma win, or a 0–0 draw. Anything to keep his octopus-hands off her.

'Go on then. What was the score?'

'5–0,' chuckles Kelly. 'And that's against the likes of Cannovaro and Lillian Thuram. World-class defenders and they couldn't live with us. Not bad, eh?'

Five! That's five hugs. I can see Fitz holding her tight. So tight. Oh God.

'We were class,' says Fitz. 'Hamann got the first. Cracker of a free kick.'

'Our new signings scored too,' says Gary. 'Barmby and McAllister got on the score sheet. We've bought some good players in the close season.'

Don't rub it in. What have we got? Just Barthez and he was left exposed all afternoon by a threadbare defence. The neon sign flashes even more intensely. December 16th. Manchester United v. Liverpool. I hear Houllier's words from the year before last: 'One day we're going to beat them.' Maybe this is the year. Armageddon.

'Who scored the other two?' I ask, dreading the answer.

Please God, not Michael Owen.

'Michael Owen,' Julie replies.

OK, ignore me then, God. Rub it in all you like.

'He's back to his best,' says Julie.

'That's right,' Kelly adds, knowing exactly which buttons to press. 'Back to his gorgeous best.'

Fitz lifts the club badge on his shirt to his lips.

'The best squad an Anfield manager's put together in ten years. We're going to slaughter you this year,' he says.

December 16th. Armageddon.

'Just watch us take that title off you.'

'I'd like to see you try,' I reply, trying my best not to pout. I do that when I'm up against it.

'Man U. have had their own way for ten years,' said Fitz, 'But look at our record. Eighteen league championships, four European Cups.'

He probably doesn't know it, but he's logging on to my worst nightmare. All good things have to come to an end. Is this the year Man U. start to slide?

'Be worried, Terry, be very worried. When it comes to winning honours, there isn't another English club comes close to us.'

'We've won the most FA Cups,' I venture.

'Yes, and we all know what you think of the Cup. You didn't even play in it last year.'

Fitz gives a broad grin. He knows that's the killer answer. Without another word he snakes his arm round Julie's waist. He's reminding me who got the girl. Julie gives me a pitying smile – at least I think that's what it is – and they walk off up the road. It has started to rain and they're sharing an umbrella.

'By the way,' shouts Fitz, 'How's it going with that skinny bird I saw you with at the school disco?'

Skinny bird! Fitz doesn't half know how to put somebody down.

'Boy, did she have the hots for you. What's her name? Yeah, Chloe.'

Julie scowls and pulls away from him. Refusing his hand, she walks off with Kelly. At least she doesn't want to join in Fitz's tormenting. Gary's another matter. Next minute he and Fitz are cooing her name:

'Chloe, Chloe.'

I ought to say something, but I don't. I just stand there, sick with powerless anger. When they get to the roundabout they're a foursome again, each couple sharing an umbrella. Julie's annoyance with Fitz hasn't lasted long. As they reach the corner, Julie glances back at me. I want to run after her and tell her she's too good for the likes of Fitz. I don't of course.

Instead, I just stand there while the pelting rain runs down my face.

3

Saturday 19th August
9.00 a.m.

'I'm making a new season's resolution,' I declare.

'What's that?' comes Bobby's voice, still thick with sleep.

I look down at him. Last night was band practice at the community centre with *The Sons of Moe Szyslak*, so he stayed the night. Now he's curled up in a sleeping bag on top of the inflatable bed. He sleeps over at mine as often as he can, usually when his mum is having her boyfriend over. You know the one, big guy, cocker spaniel. Bobby doesn't like him. The big guy, that is. He doesn't mind the cocker spaniel.

'No more divided loyalties,' I tell him. 'I'm going to stop thinking about Julie and just have the best time with Chloe.'

I've been thinking about this ever since the drumming rain woke me up about an hour ago.

'Good for you,' says Bobby.

What he means is: shut up and let me sleep. Bobby doesn't believe in crawling out of bed until eleven o'clock at the earliest. It's a habit he's developed while he's been off school. That way he avoids having breakfast with the big guy and his cocker spaniel. The big guy has bad breath and the cocker spaniel has fleas.

'I mean, Chloe's a lovely girl,' I say. 'You've said so yourself.'

'Yes, lovely,' grunts Bobby, burying his head in the sleeping bag.

'And Julie doesn't even know I exist.'

I can't help wanting Bobby to contradict me, remind me how she came up to me outside the house that time, how she smiled at me in the canteen, how she pulled her hand out of

85

Fitz's when he was tormenting me. He doesn't say a word. Instead he yawns and rolls over. I stare at him in his sleeping bag, a shiny, red caterpillar on the floor.

'Are you listening to me?'

'Yeah, course I am. You're going to stop thinking about Chloe and make a go of it with Julie.'

I give an exasperated cry and boot the misshapen red caterpillar. Bobby corrects himself.

'Sorry, reverse that. Chloe yes, Julie no. She's a Scouser, she must go.'

He pokes his head out of the sleeping bag, very pleased with himself.

'Hey, I'm a poet and I didn't know it.'

'You're a wombat.'

Bobby scratches his head and sits up.

'I'm a hungry wombat. Is your mum in?'

'No, she's taken Amy to some horse thing. One of those gymkhanas. My dad's gone with them.'

Bobby's pulling on his jogging pants.

'Does that mean anything?'

'What, like them getting back together, you mean?'

Bobby nods.

'No chance. They're just putting on a show for Amy.'

'So we've got the house to ourselves?'

'Uh huh.'

'Well, you know what that means, Terry lad,' he says, pulling on his Adidas top. 'Monster breakfast coming up.'

Twenty minutes later we're wolfing down eggs, bacon and pancakes with Canadian maple syrup. Bobby even dips his bacon in maple syrup and runny egg!

'You're disgusting,' I tell him.

'No, I'm not.'

Twin streams of runny egg and maple syrup are spilling down his chin. Rather than watch his disgusting eating habits, I glance out of the window. The rainclouds are clearing and the sun is peeping out.

'Good conditions for the big kick-off,' I say.

Man U. don't play until tomorrow but I can feel the tremor of excitement. The butterflies. I glance at the clock. This time last season, Dad and I were getting ready to steam down the M62. Even when United aren't playing, there's plenty to think about, psyching myself up, willing our closest rivals to trip up. This afternoon I'll be flitting from Century 105 to Sky's Soccer Saturday, willing Sunderland to beat Arsenal, Bradford to beat Liverpool, West Ham to beat Chelsea, Everton to beat Leeds. As if he's just read my thoughts, Bobby chips in with:

'We could do you a favour this afternoon at Leeds.'

I grin. Bobby's a staunch Evertonian and it seems cruel to remind him that Everton have only won once at Elland Road since the end of World War Two. Hitler's got a better chance, and he's dead!

'Chance would be a fine thing.'

No, come ten to five the classified results will register wins for all the bad guys, leaving us with a job to do against Newcastle. I try to focus on Chloe and Man U., but for some reason a snowstorm of other images fills my mind: Julie in her leotard; *This is Anfield*; Fitz in his Liverpool home strip; *You'll Never Walk Alone*; Julie at the disco with her head on Fitz's shoulder; Liverpool and their eighteen league championships and four European cups; Julie in her little black dress.

Julie, always Julie.

I clear the breakfast things, feeling like I'm letting Chloe down already, and give a long sigh.

'No wonder people break resolutions.'

Saturday 19th August
3.15 p.m.

Bobby and I are squatting on the wooden floor. There are four empty cans of Red Bull and two screwed up packets of Monster Munch in the waste paper bin. You've got to keep up your energy levels when you're listening to football.

'Is this the way you imagined spending your Saturday afternoons?' I ask, insanely jealous of the hundreds of thousands of fans watching their teams on the first day of the season.

'Pretty much,' says Bobby. 'Only I didn't expect Chloe to turn up.'

'What?'

I see a fuzz of red hair at the window and hear the doorbell.

'Wonder what she wants?' I murmur.

'You, you sexy devil,' says Bobby.

He does this low growl just to wind me up.

'You can cut that out,' I tell him as I go to answer the door.

'Hi Terry,' says Chloe. 'Doing anything?'

Her eyes light up the moment she sees me. I wish I could return the compliment, but right now she isn't really welcome. I don't tell her. I'm too much of a coward for that.

'No, Bobby and I are just hanging out listening to the match reports.'

Her eyes dull a little at the mention of Bobby. I told her Mum and Amy were going to be out so she obviously thought she'd have me to herself. Bobby curses loudly in the living room.

'Go on,' I say, 'What's happened?'

'Leeds 1, Everton 0,' he reports.

'Oh wonderful!'

'Why are you bothered?' asks Chloe. 'I thought you supported Man. United.'

'I do,' I explain. 'Leeds are one of our rivals for the Premiership.'

Chloe's *Oh* of bewilderment reminds me she knows nothing about football, and cares even less. Try as I might, I can't stop Julie from popping into my head. She would never ask a question like that. She understands football. Minutes later the afternoon gets worse. Chelsea take the lead against West Ham.

'Is that bad?' asks Chloe.

Don't snap, I tell myself.

'Yes Chloe,' I tell her, desperately trying to shoo Julie out of my head. 'It's bad.'

Bad becomes disastrous for both me and Bobby just before half time. Leeds have gone 2–0 up.

Bobby sits dejectedly on the floor with his face buried in his hands.

'What's the matter with him?' Chloe whispers.

'It's called pain,' I explain, just about keeping control of my temper. 'All summer he's lived for today, just waiting for

Everton to put on a good performance on the opening Saturday.'

'It's only a game,' says Chloe.

That does it. Julie won't be shooed. She would never say anything as dumb as that. She's got Shankly's words carved onto her heart:

Football is not a matter of life and death; it's much more important than that.

I see Julie next to Fitz at the Anfield Road End. The pair of them are wearing matching Liverpool home shirts. I glance at the scores in the right hand corner of the TV screen. At least they're not winning yet. At eight minutes past four there is actually a piece of good news.

Paolo Di Canio has equalised for West Ham against Chelsea. Seven minutes later it gets even better. Sunderland have taken the lead against Arsenal. Maybe this Saturday afternoon can be salvaged after all.

'Can't we go out somewhere?' asks Chloe.

'I can't go out now,' I tell her, appalled at the idea. 'You've heard the scores, haven't you?'

'Yes,' says Chloe, all sweetness and light. 'And it won't make any difference you being stuck in front of the TV.'

The words are no sooner out of her mouth than Chelsea retake the lead. I just stop myself from saying:

Now look what you've done.

I've hardly got over that disappointment when even worse news come through. Liverpool have taken the lead against Bradford. Bobby groans and buries his head even deeper in his hands. He hates Liverpool almost as much as I do. As far as he's concerned there are only two teams on Merseyside, Everton and Everton reserves.

'Now what's up with him?' asks Chloe.

'His team are losing 2–0,' I explain, wondering if she's trying to be stupid, or if it comes naturally. 'And the old enemy across Stanley Park are winning.'

Chloe gives another of her *Oh*s.

By full-time, the news is almost universally bleak. Liverpool, Leeds and Chelsea have all won. The only shaft of sunlight is the news that Arsenal have gone down 1–0 and their star midfielder Patrick Vieira has been sent off.

'Come on now,' says Chloe, 'After all, it's only the first match.'

Bobby reacts as if somebody's slipped a firecracker down his pants. He shoots up and bolts for the hallway.

'I'm off home,' he says.

I follow him to the front door.

'Did you hear that?' he hisses, mimicking her slightly reedy voice. '*It's only the first match*. Typical comment from a female.'

I give a sympathetic smile.

'She means well.'

'Yes? Well, so did Genghis Khan. So did the rotten Spanish Inquisition. Terry, forget the resolution. The girl knows nothing about football. Julie yes, Chloe no, she's a dufus, she must go.'

Suddenly, despite all my efforts, Julie's face is looming larger than ever.

4

'Isn't Chloe a lovely girl?' says Mum.

She's talked about nothing else since yesterday. She and Amy came in from the gymkhana and caught me and Chloe kissing. Oddly enough, she didn't seem bothered. In fact, she seemed chuffed to bits. Somehow, she's got it into her head that if I'm going out with a *Nice Girl* – and as she keeps telling everyone Chloe's a *very* nice girl – then I'll let my hair grow again and be a *Nice Boy*. I don't quite know why, but if you've got a Number One haircut, it's route one to hell for you, my lad. After ten minutes of Mum interrogating me about Chloe, I'm high-tailing it to Bobby's for some light relief. There's no better way to warm up for this afternoon's match than a kick around. We recruit a few lads from up the street and head for the field. It's attack and defend with me in goal.

'Fabien Barthez!' I roar, the first time I make a decent save.

'You've certainly got the haircut for it,' says Bobby.

I pull a face and lob the ball out.

'Hey, look who's here,' says Bobby, as he measures up to defend the goal.

It's Julie and Kelly. Julie's in a purple Ellesse dress and white trainers. It's her legs I notice most. They're sun-tanned, and they shine. I don't really register what Kelly's wearing. Something Sabrina-ish.

'Hello boys,' says Kelly.

There's a sarcastic sting in the tail of her *hello*. Julie gives a winsome smile. I get the weirdest feeling the smile is for me. Or is that wishful thinking? I wish some scientist would invent the Fancy-ometer, cast-iron proof of how a girl feels about you.

It would save a lot of embarrassing moments. Julie and Kelly stop to watch us for a few minutes.

That's my cue to launch myself into some spectacular saves. I'm out to impress the girl. I tip one shot over the bar with my fingertips. At least I would have done if there was a bar. Then I palm another away round the right hand post. Or, to put it another way, the right hand rolled-up sweater. Finally, I dive low to smother Bobby's drive, skidding across the uneven grass surface. Julie's impressed. She can't take her eyes off me. All of a sudden, I'm swelling up like a puffer fish.

She's looking at me. Julie's actually got her eye on me.

Bobby fishes a bottle of Fanta out of his bag.

'Five minute break,' he says, passing the bottle round.

I take a swig and turn to Julie.

'How's it going?'

'Good.'

'Did you go to the match yesterday?'

Julie nods.

Please, not with Fitz. Frisky Fitzy with his octopus hands.

'I went with my Dad and the boys.'

That's music to my ears. It gives me the confidence to make a joke.

'What, Huey, Duey and Louis?'

Julie giggles and Kelly gives her a sideways glance as if to ask what she's playing at. This is going well.

'Yes, that's them.'

I look into her brown eyes. They're sparkling and there are these cute little wrinkles round the corners where she's smiling. This is going really well. What I don't get is why Julie and Kelly seem to be looking at my chest all the time. It's not like I've got any pecs to speak of.

'I listened to the reports on Sky,' I tell her. 'Rodney Marsh called it a 1–0 massacre.'

'That about sums it up,' says Julie. 'We were all over them like a rash. Just couldn't get it in the net. Good strike by Heskey though.'

'Yes, I saw it on Match of the Day.'

I resist the tendency to congratulate him for staying on his feet for once. This is going *so* well. It's like Fitz doesn't exist. Or Chloe. I start to feel guilty, but Julie's smiling face soon puts that right. When I'm talking to her there doesn't seem to be another human being on the planet. I just wish I knew why she keeps looking at my chest.

'Still in the gym club?' I ask.

It's a way of fishing for a progress report on her and Fitz. I remember that Fitz's kid sister's in the same club.

'Mm,' says Julie. 'We've started training three times a week, Tuesday, Thursday and Saturday.'

I know I shouldn't, but I mentally note the days.

'We're away in the Isle of Man for four days next week.'

Good. That's four days away from Fitz. I'm searching for something clever to say when Kelly sticks her oar in.

'How's Chloe?' she asks acidly. Though her family moved up the hill out of Liverpool when she was five, Kelly's your ultimate Scouse nationalist. She doesn't want her best mate getting chatted up by a Manc. The interruption earns her a glare from me and Julie. There's definitely something in the air, a connection, an electricity. I'm not imagining it. Please tell me I'm not imagining it.

'Fine,' I mumble.

The spell is broken and Julie starts to go.

'See you,' she says.

'Yes, see you.'

As they carry on across the field, ponytails bobbing, Bobby offers me the Fanta.

'She's such a nice girl,' I say, 'Too good for Fitz.'

'You still fancy her rotten, don't you?' says Bobby, digging me in the ribs.

I nod, which makes me feel even guiltier. What about my resolution? What about Chloe? But there's no sense in lying to Bobby. He's known me since we were in the nursery, fighting in the sandpit.

'And I suppose you think that went well?' he says.

I'm thinking me and Julie in matching pullovers pushing a trolley round the supermarket.

'Yes. Why, don't you?'

'I've just one word to say to you,' says Bobby. 'Dog poop.'

'What?'

I look down. To my horror, there it is a huge streak of the stuff right across the front of my new Asics top. I must have dived right into a big, steaming pile of it when I made that last save.

'Oh gross!'

Then I think of Julie staring at it while I rabbit on with this big, stupid grin on my face. No wonder she was staring at my chest. It was poop, not pecs, she was looking at.

'Oh God!'

I sink to my knees. There's me thinking she's smiling at me and all the time she's laughing at my pooped-on shirt. What an idiot!

'Why didn't you warn me?'

'What was I supposed to do? You wouldn't have thanked me for pointing it out while you were chatting up the lovely Julie.'

Julie and me and the dog poop makes three.

Ohmigod, ohmigod, ohmigod.

'I suppose that's the end of the game,' says Bobby. 'You'll be attracting too many flies.'

I hold the ball to my chest in a vain attempt to hide the stain.

'You're not kidding. I've got to go home to change.'

We leave the other boys at the top of Bobby's street and head for my house.

'You seem to have forgotten Chloe pretty quickly,' says Bobby.

'No, I haven't!'

Bobby's struck a chord.

'It isn't going far if your heart isn't in it,' says Bobby, sounding more like an agony aunt all the time. (Do they have agony uncles?)

'My heart *is* in it,' I tell him.

I try to sound convincing but it doesn't wash with Bobby.

'Yes? Tell it to the marines. This is your best mate you're talking to. I can read you like a book.'

I blush right to the top of my ears. Bobby's got me sussed, all right. But Julie and I are going nowhere, especially after the dog poop incident.

'I'm sticking with Chloe, all right?' I answer hotly.

'Whatever you say,' Bobby replies. 'Just do one thing for me. Tell me you're over Julie.'

I try to get the words out, but I can't. Instead I do what I always do when he's got one over on me. I insult him.

'Bobby, you're stupid.'

But he isn't. Not by a long chalk.

Sunday 20th August
4.00 p.m.

Yesterday counts as Amy Access, so today it's just me and Dad and the TV set. Mum told me to enjoy the match. Just goes to show she doesn't really understand about football. Enjoy definitely isn't the right word. From the moment I get up in the morning my whole system is turned upside down. Fear of losing is like a stream of hot lava bubbling through my veins. I spend the whole match on the edge of my seat, willing every opposition attack to break down, every United move to end in a goal. Today the stakes are high. We looked sluggish in the Charity Shield against Chelsea and yesterday all but one of our title rivals won well. Only Arsenal stumbled at Sunderland. We can't afford to drop points.

'Just look at that,' says Dad approvingly as the team take the field. 'Sixty-seven thousand fans packed into the Theatre of Dreams.'

I can't help but have a dig.

'Just a pity we're not among them,' I say.

Dad takes it on the chin. The tension eases as United launch attack after attack on the Newcastle goal.

'They're looking sharp,' says Dad, offering the Pringles.

'Yes, they're up for it.'

Just how up for it we discover in the twenty-first minute. Stam almost scores from a corner. A second corner on the run finds Ronny Johnsen clear and he heads home. Dad and I are on our feet, arms raised. It's almost like being at Old Trafford.

Almost.

We continue to pile on the pressure and when Giggsy is brought down in the penalty area we're screaming for a penalty.

'The only thing that worries me,' I tell Dad, 'is that we've had so many chances but are still only 1–0 up. It only takes one mistake and they're right back in it.'

Dad nods.

But in the seventieth minute I can finally breathe easily. Cole and Giggs exchange a neat one-two and Andy Cole fires the ball into the far corner.

'2–0,' chuckles Dad. 'Game, set and match.'

Thank goodness for that. If I bump into Fitz I can hold my head up. My mind is already fixed on the coming week. Liverpool visit Arsenal on Monday. We go to Ipswich on Tuesday. With a bit of luck we'll be three points clear of the old enemy by ten o'clock Tuesday night. But just when everything's rosy, the phone rings.

'Hello,' says Dad. 'Oh hi.'

There's something about his voice that makes me sit up and take notice.

'Yes, I'll see you there. Eight o'clock.'

Dad glances at me then speaks again.

'Looking forward to it.'

His eyes are still on me. He's expecting the third degree but I don't ask him who it was on the phone. I'm not stupid. I know it was a woman.

'Anyway,' I say, 'I'm getting off.'

'OK son,' says Dad.

I think he's relieved. He doesn't fancy explaining the mystery caller, and I'm in no hurry to find out. As I hit the street, I fish for some change in my pockets. I think I'll buy Mum a packet of Hobnobs on the way home.

Tuesday 22nd August
6.00 p.m.

It's boys' night. Me and Bobby playing badminton. I've spent the day with Chloe at Croxteth Park. Bobby was out with Rosie last night, and he and Caitlin tagged along to Croccy with us this afternoon. So we're getting a break from the girls. It's just the two of us knocking the shuttlecock back and forth. I glance around the main hall. There are three activities going on at the same time. It's judo club nearest the door, the badminton club in the middle, but it's the far end of the hall that concerns me. Behind this big partition net everything is set up for the gymnastics club. Yes, you've got it, it's Julie's gym club. Maybe I'm a pathetic loser, but I just couldn't stay away.

'Hey Terry, pay attention,' says Bobby.

He's just whipped the shuttlecock past me.

'Sorry.'

I hear the door creak. It's two girls in tracksuits. They head for the gym area and unzip their jackets. Bobby follows them with his eyes.

'Hey you,' I say, 'Aren't two girls enough for you?'

'Terry,' he replies, 'there aren't enough girls in the world for me.'

I swat the shuttlecock back at him and he grins broadly. Ever since he got off with Rosie he thinks he's God's gift to women. The grin fades a little the next time the door opens. In walk Julie, Kelly and Pepsey Cooper. I avoid Bobby's inquiring glance.

'Come on,' I say, 'Let's play.'

In the corner of my eye I glimpse the three girls whispering. They're staring in my direction.

'So that's your little game,' says Bobby knowingly.

'What are you on about?'

'Oh, come on, do you think I was born yesterday?'

More members of the gym club arrive, maybe twenty in all. The gymnasts are warming up. Julie's wearing a white leotard with a blue star on the shoulder. Her hair is done up in a matching scrunchie. I'm finding it impossible to look away. This is what eyes are made for.

'Terry.'

Bobby's hissing at me.

'What?'

It's Fitz. He's just come in with his little sister, Hayley. He's telling her he'll pick her up in two hours when he spots me. Instinctively he looks over at Julie.

'What are you doing here, Payne?'

He says *Payne*, not *Terry*. There's no love lost. I brandish the badminton racket.

'What does it look like?'

'You know what I mean.'

He gives me a venomous look then goes over to Julie. They exchange a few words. I know what he's doing. He's saying: *She's mine.* That's a red rag to a bull. I hit him with the only weapon at hand, Liverpool's 2–0 defeat last night at Arsenal.

'So what was the score, Fitzy?'

'Get stuffed.'

I remember the way he wound me up over the Charity Shield. It's pay-back time.

'Two players sent off. You're hardly going to win the Fair Play award, are you?'

'The ref was a crackpot,' says Fitz, really rattled. 'He ruined the game.'

'Oh yes,' I answer. 'It's always the ref's fault, isn't it? Funny that, I thought it was because you played like a pub side.'

Fitz gives me a daggers look and walks up to me. For an instant I think he's going to swing for me. But that's not his intention. Instead he shoves his face right into mine.

'At least I'm not some saddo who hangs round somebody else's girlfriend,' he hisses.

'I'm here to play badminton,' I tell him, trying not to show he's got to me.

'Sure, and it's just a coincidence you booked the court when Julie's here. Kelly was right. You're a lousy stalker. At least you can't follow Julie round for a while. She's off to the Isle of Man for a week. Bet you didn't know I'd be going with her.'

I feel a knife going through my heart.

'That's right, when our Hayley goes to a display the whole family goes with her. We make a holiday of it. What do you think of that, Terry, me and Julie in the Isle of Man for four days. Sun, sea, sand and . . . well, I'll leave that to your imagination.'

I know there's nothing in it. He's just boasting, but my mind is working overtime. Suddenly, it's *Titanic* just before the iceberg hits, with Julie as Kate Winslet and Fitz as Leonardo Di Caprio. He knows he's scored a direct hit.

'Jealous, are we?'

I shove him away. He reacts by raising a hand. For a moment

I think it's going to turn into a punch-up, then Fitz gives his superior grin.

'What's the point in hitting you?' he says. 'Julie isn't interested anyway. See you, saddo.'

I'm dying to hit him with a stinging put-down but I can't think of a single thing to say. As Fitz walks past the judo club he gives his parting shot:

'You know, maybe I should tell that skinny bird of yours what you're like. Yes, I'm sure Chloe would be really interested.'

I pull a face but I don't feel too good the way things have turned out. I feel even worse when I see Julie peering through the partition netting. She shakes her head and returns to her warm-up exercises.

Tuesday 22nd August
8.00 p.m.

'Well,' says Bobby sarcastically. 'That went well.'

'Oh, knock it off.'

'No, I thought you handled yourself really well.'

'Bobby, shut up. I'm not trying to chat Julie up. I'm not a two-timer. Not like some.'

He ignores the dig.

'No? And what if Julie showed some interest?'

'I'm going out with Chloe. Full stop. End of story.'

If only. Why does everything have to be so complicated? I mean, why can't I just shut Julie out of my mind and settle for what I've got? What's so all-fired difficult about that? I turn my key in the front door and walk into the hallway. Bobby's right, of course. Turning up on Julie's gym night was really stupid, just like going to the pony sanctuary that time. On both occasions I was asking for it and I got it. Julie's with Fitz. All I've done is make sure she stays with him. Talk about own goals.

'That you, Terry?' calls Mum.

'No,' I answer. 'The Boston Strangler.'

'There's a plate of sandwiches for you and Bobby,' says Mum, ignoring the flip reply. 'I assume he's with you.'

'Hi, Mrs Payne,' says Bobby brightly.

'Hi Bobby.'

He tucks into the sandwiches while I turn on the radio. We're playing Ipswich. 7.45 p.m. kick-off so by now we should be 1–0 up at least.

'And Beckham's bringing the ball away,' says the commentator. 'United are still trying to get back on level terms.'

I stare at the radio in disbelief. What's going on? We can't be losing, not to a bunch of turnip-heads! No, I've heard it wrong. Must have.

'Just to remind you of the surprise scoreline,' come the chilling words. 'Ipswich are 1–0 up against the Champions.'

Bobby sprays sandwich crumbs all over the table.

'You're losing,' he says. 'To flipping Ipswich?'

Suddenly I can't eat. The news has me pacing up and down the kitchen. Not only are we losing, we're getting overrun in midfield. Well, thanks a bunch United, I was relying on you to cheer me up after what happened at the leisure centre, and this is what you do to me. The minutes tick by and we only have one decent effort on goal.

'Oh, come on lads,' I say, 'You should be stuffing this shower.'

But they're stuffing us. It's been a night for stuffing. Fitz stuffed me at the leisure centre, stuffed me good style. Julie's face told me that much. Finally, seven minutes before half-time, we draw level. Beckham puts in a free kick and Wallwork dummies the ball. A soft goal but they all count. I feel a huge sense of relief. We'll walk it in the second half.

'So what happened to the new season's resolution?' asks Bobby, tucking into the cookies during the interval. 'What happened to I'm not dumping Chloe?'

'I'm not.'

'No, but you can't get the lovely Julie out of your head, can you?'

'Leave it, eh?'

'Sure, it's your problem.'

Too right. And so are United. In the second half they never quite get going and it stays at 1–1.

'Disappointing result,' observes Bobby at the final whistle.

100

'Yes,' I say. 'Sometimes things don't turn out the way they're supposed to.'

I think about Julie. Then I remember Fitz's threat to grass me up to Chloe.

Do they ever?

5

Dad's just been to pick up Amy. He's taking her and her friend Katie swimming. He asked if I wanted to come. I told him I was seeing Chloe. He doesn't argue or look disappointed. I think he's relieved. He's long since run out of original places to go.

'Did I hear you say you were seeing Chloe?' asks Mum.

' 'S'right.'

I emit the lowest teengrunt I can manage. Does she have to harass me like this?

'Going somewhere nice?'

Time for teengrunt two.

'Dunno. Just out.'

The doorbell rings.

'Oh, hello Chloe love,' says Mum.

Could she be more gushy? I'm half-expecting her to cut cucumber sandwiches and pour ginger beer.

'Hi, Mrs Payne,' says Chloe.

She sounds like she's glad to see Mum. How do people do that? How do they make everybody they meet feel important?

'Are we going?' I ask.

I feel tetchy and on edge. I can't get Fitz's threat out of my mind.

'OK.'

The moment we hit the street Chloe starts going on about how nice my mum is and what a shame people have to split up and don't I think honesty matters in a relationship. Guilt-mites are burrowing under my skin.

'I don't know how you can cover for Bobby the way you do.'

I stop dead.

'You know about Bobby?'

'I know he's seeing somebody. I think Caitlin does too.'

'But how?'

I suddenly realise I've just confirmed her suspicions.

'Just the way he acts,' says Chloe. 'He's a player.'

'You've been watching too many American chat shows,' I tell her.

I see her on an imaginary TV screen. Go Ricky, go Ricky.

'But I'm right, aren't I? He *is* seeing somebody else?'

We've reached Eccleston Street. We've been going nowhere in particular and ended up in the town centre.

'Promise you won't say anything to Caitlin.'

'Of course not. That's up to Bobby.'

'He met this girl on work experience, Rosie.'

Chloe shakes her head slowly.

'I think that's disgusting, don't you?'

It's like Fitzy is right here with us. This little Fitzy-devil is perched on Chloe's shoulder grinning at me, enjoying my discomfort.

'Terry?'

'What?'

'Don't you think it's awful when people cheat?'

The guilt-mites are making my skin crawl.

'Oh yeah, awful.'

I mustn't have sounded too convincing because Chloe continues the interrogation. All she needs now is an angle-poise lamp and a set of thumbscrews. Ve haf vays of making you squirm.

'You wouldn't ever do that to me, would you?'

By now it feels like the guilt-mites are drawing blood.

'No, never.'

'It would break my heart if you weren't honest with me.'

It's quiet at this end of the street. I pull her to me and plant a kiss on her lips. The next moment we're kissing hard, lips slightly parted. She doesn't know I did it to shut her up. She thinks I'm being romantic. In fact, I'm being desperate.

Saturday 26th August
2.30 p.m.

I wouldn't normally be out so close to kick-off, but I've got to warn Bobby that Caitlin's suspicious. OK, so he's been asking for it, but he's still my mate. I knock on the door. Bobby's mum answers. A cocker spaniel is scrabbling to push past her and jump on me. The big boyfriend must be there.

'Is Bobby in?'

'He's in his room.'

She turns and shouts up the stairs.

'Bobby, it's Terry.'

I climb the stairs wondering just how to break the news without incriminating myself.

'All right, Terry,' he says.

I look round the room. There are apple cores, yoghurt cartons and sweet wrappers everywhere. I shove two pizza boxes off a beanbag and sit down.

'Didn't expect you,' says Bobby. 'I thought you were out with Chloe.'

'I was. I came to tell you something.'

'Yes?'

'Caitlin's on to you.'

Bobby laughs.

'That all? So what's new? She's been quizzing me all week.'

'What did you say?'

'Nothing.'

I stare at him.

'How can you be so cool about it?'

'So she finds out. I've still got Rosie.'

'Bobby, you're disgusting.'

'Says who?'

'Chloe . . . and me.'

Bobby laughs again.

'You don't sound too sure.'

'Sure I'm sure.'

I want to be like Chloe, one hundred per cent sure of how she feels. I'm trying to take the moral high ground, but it isn't easy when you're sinking into a beanbag.

'You ought to be faithful to one person, honest. You shouldn't cheat.'

'Who's that talking? You or Chloe?'

I get annoyed.

'Me, you lower life-form. I've always thought that.'

Bobby chuckles.

'Not a very good example of it though, are you?'

'Meaning?'

'Meaning there are things I could tell Chloe.'

I blush.

'No, there aren't! I've never gone out with anybody else. Not even kissed anyone else. She's the first one, the *only* one.'

'OK, so maybe you haven't actually gone out with anyone else, but you'd like to.'

'The difference between me and you,' I retort hotly, 'is that I can control myself.'

Bobby roars with laughter. I feel totally stupid. I have this picture of myself as a demented professor wrestling with a rebellious robot hand: I CAN control myself!

'Honestly Terry, you take everything so seriously. You sound like a middle-aged man.'

He looks at his watch.

'Here's something you should take seriously. It's kick-off in ten minutes. If we go now we can listen to the footy round yours.'

'Why not here?'

'Slughead's here.'

I frown. Slughead?

'Mum's boyfriend.'

Of course. Big guy. Cocker spaniel. Slughead.

'Ours it is.'

Saturday 26th August
3.30 p.m.

It's mixed fortunes so far. Bobby and I have got good reason to be happy. Both Man U. and Everton are winning, but so are Leeds, Arsenal and Liverpool.

To make matters worse, Michael Owen's scored for Liverpool. Out on the Isle of Man, Julie and Fitz are probably hugging each other in celebration right now. Unfortunately, Chloe just came round so we're having to put up with her interruptions. When the Owen goal went in I cursed loudly.

'I didn't know you swore,' said Chloe, disapprovingly.

What is it with her? Does she have to be Miss Nice from Nice Avenue, Nicetown? Bobby is taking care not to look at her. Every time their eyes meet she gives him this searing glare.

She's definitely got him down as a love-rat. When Bobby goes to the toilet, she whispers into my ear:

'I think he's a bad influence. You act differently when he's around.'

When Chloe goes to get a can of Coke, Bobby whispers into my ear:

'She's going to make you as boring as she is.'

He mimics her voice:

'Terry, I didn't know you swore.'

I laugh, which makes Chloe scowl when she comes back with the Coke. Andy Cole makes up for it at West Ham. He's just put us 2–0 up. Everton are 2–0 up as well. Unfortunately, Liverpool have just taken a 3–0 lead.

'Why does it bother you so much if Liverpool are winning?' asks Chloe.

She sounds genuinely bewildered.

'They're the enemy,' I explain.

Of course, I don't explain about Julie and Fitz.

'It *is* only a game,' says Chloe.

Just how much it isn't a game she discovers in the closing stages of the second half. Everton squander their 2–0 lead against Derby.

Bobby starts calling his players all the names under the sun. Then in the final three minutes we throw it away as well, having to settle for a 2–2 draw. The only saving grace of a disappointing afternoon is that Liverpool have drawn as well, surrendering a three-goal lead to draw 3–3. Dad arrives with Amy and Katie. Stevie Wonder's 'Superstition' is playing. I tell him the score.

'We've got to do something about that defence,' he says, shaking his head. 'Fancy squandering a 2–0 lead.'

'We did the same,' says Bobby. 'Anyway, I'm getting off, Terry.'

'See you, Bobby.'

Chloe stands on the doorstep with her arms folded. She doesn't say anything to him.

'I thought I might come round tomorrow,' I say, decided to be nice to Dad. 'Watch the Celtic–Rangers game with you.'

Dad grimaces.

'Sorry son,' he says. 'I've got plans.'

I see Mum looking through the net curtains at us. I know exactly what plans he means.

'Who is she?' I ask.

'You'll meet her soon enough. I'll be in touch, Terry.'

'Yes, see you Dad.'

Chloe has been listening. Later, when we're alone she says:

'First Bobby, now your dad. You wouldn't treat me like that, would you Terry?'

No Chloe, I never will. I've made up my mind. Come the start of a school year I'm not going to so much as look at Julie. The funny thing is, I can't quite come up with the right words to reassure Chloe. For the second time that day I can only think of one way to answer. I kiss her.

PART THREE

The Girl
or
Belgian Suicide

1

There's a kind of grudging admiration in Bobby's voice.

'I never thought you'd make it this far.'

Neither did I. We've been going out for nearly six weeks. We've started a new term together, moved up to Year 11 together, everything we've done together.

'I've told you, haven't I?' I say. 'It's me and Chloe, full stop, end of story. We're together.' We've just left Chloe and Caitlin at the bus stop. This afternoon is strictly boys only. We're going round to Dad's flat to watch the England–Germany game.

'And you never give Julie a second's thought?'

I couldn't say that. In fact, I find myself thinking about her most of the time. It's not like I ask her in, she just strolls through the back door of my mind. The last few weeks haven't been easy, watching her and Fitz talking in the canteen or the library, heads so close together they almost touch. But I've pretended not to notice. By steering clear of Julie, I may even have salvaged a little of my dignity.

'I'm with Chloe.'

Bobby smiles in that superior way of his.

'Let's get our skates on,' I say. 'We're going to miss the kick-off at this rate.'

Of course, there's no chance of that happening. Bobby takes the hint: time to talk about something else.

'What's your prediction?' he asks.

'Score draw.'

'You're kidding! Did you see Germany at Euro 2000?'

'Did you see *us*?'

'Yes, but we've picked up since. Remember the friendly against France? That was a new beginning.'

I'd love to believe that, but I'm a bit short on optimism just lately. United have gone three games without a win. It's the first time that's happened since 1992. We're actually in third place in our group of the Champions' League. It doesn't bode well for England when you think the four United lads are the spine of the national team.

'We'll see.'

We invest in a bag of sweets and jog up the stairs to the flat. The door opens and we come face to face with a blond woman in her early forties. I check the leather trousers and short bomber jacket and exchange glances with Bobby.

'Mutton dressed as lamb,' I sneer as she clatters downstairs on stiletto heels.

'More like mutton dressed as mutton,' says Bobby, eager to back me up.

That's when Dad appears. He gives us daggers. He obviously heard the exchange.

'That your new squeeze?' asks Bobby.

I wince. The last thing I want to hear about right now is Dad's *squeeze*.

'That's Muriel,' says Dad.

He looks about as uncomfortable as you can get without bathing in cold baked beans. It's the first time I've run into this Muriel, though I have found evidence of her from time to time. There was hairspray in the bathroom, a pair of tights stuffed behind a cushion and a bottle of nail varnish on the coffee table. She was in quite a hurry to leave. Looks like Dad was trying to chase her out before we arrived.

'Anyway, come in lads. Make yourselves at home.'

I look round the living room for any evidence of Muriel's latest stay. There isn't any, not even a lipstick mark on the mugs.

'So how'd you meet her, Geoff?' asks Bobby.

I glare at him. He grins back in mock-innocence.

'We go to the same gym,' says Dad, taking a few Red Bulls out of the fridge and shaking out a king-size tub of Pringles into a bowl. 'We got talking and kind of clicked . . .'

112

He sees the expression on my face and trails off.

'So what's the scoreline going to be, lads?'

'I say 2–1,' says Bobby. 'Terry's going for a draw.'

'A draw? Come on, Terry, you've got to be positive. Beckham, Scholes and Cole. That's worth a goal or two.'

I shrug. I'm in no mood to banter with him. I'm still gagging on that woman's scent. Mum would have hated her. Muriel looked an inch or two taller and nearly a stone lighter.

'Oh, you've got to be kidding!'

Bobby's exclamation breaks the silence.

'What's the matter?'

'Have you heard Keegan's team selection? Southgate in midfield. What's he doing *there*? Why not give Joe Cole a chance? We need to be creative.'

Dad nods, still giving me the occasional wary glance.

'The fellow can't make his mind up. One minute it's Kev the Cavalier, then it's Mr Defensive. There's no pattern to his management.'

Dad's right there. There's no pattern to England's play, either. For the first ten minutes the Germans waltz round us. Then, on fourteen minutes, Hamann puts a free kick past Seaman.

'Where was the wall?' Bobby demands, 'Where was the flipping wall?'

'Where was the keeper?' asks Dad.

I just sit munching a chunk of chocolate. I told them.

'Might have guessed it'd be a Liverpool player who put us one down,' rants Dad.

I feel like pointing out that, as a German, Hamann is supposed to score against us. Only a Man U. fan could manage to blame Liverpool for this fiasco, but, what the heck, anything to take a pop at the Scousers! For the rest of the first half, we slip and slide in the mud. Michael Owen is particularly useless. He's like a schoolboy running round aimlessly while the big German defenders look on, completely untroubled. Bobby's so gutted by the performance he sits out the final ten minutes of the half open-mouthed, the same Pringle perched unchewed on his lower lip.

'Rubbish,' he announces when the half-time whistles blows. 'Utter flipping rubbish.'

Nobody's arguing. There isn't even an inquest during the interval. When Bobby goes for a pee, Dad leans across.

'Sorry about Muriel,' he says. 'I meant to have her out of here before you arrived.'

'Forget it,' I say. 'No skin off my nose.'

'I just wanted . . .'

'Leave it, Dad,' I tell him. 'It's your life. You can do what you want with it.'

And that's the cue for Bobby to return.

'At least it can't get any worse,' he says, oblivious to the tension between us.

True, but it doesn't get much better. Becks plays himself into the ground and comes close to equalising. When he limps off with a knee injury, England's last hope goes with him. At the final whistle, Bobby and I bombard the TV screen with Pringles.

'Hang on there, lads,' says Dad. 'It's me that has to clean this lot up.'

Bobby gives him a long, hard look.

'You mean you clean up?'

'Of course I do.'

'Funny,' says Bobby. 'I thought men only did that to impress women.'

He sees me looking at him, and remembers Muriel.

'Oh yeah, I forgot.'

Saturday 7th October
6.00 p.m.

Even Bobby isn't insensitive enough to mention Muriel in front of Mum, so when we get back to my house, he restricts himself to a few comments about England's performance. He even asks Mum if she's lost weight.

'I wish,' she says. 'With my diets, it's a case of one pound off, two pounds back.'

'What was that about?' I ask Bobby when we get to my room.

'Come again?'

'Asking my mum if she's lost weight. You know she hasn't.'

'Dunno. I suppose I felt sorry for her. Something to do with seeing that Muriel.'

'What did you think of her?'

'Sad old slapper,' says Bobby, never one to be too subtle. 'See that tan? Straight out of a bottle.'

'Mm,' I say. 'But you can see why Dad likes her. I mean, you can tell she works out.'

Bobby nods and traces an hourglass figure with his hands.

'Doesn't look like your folks will be getting back together, does it?'

'No.'

'I told you what it would be like, Terry lad.'

'Yes, I know. Stuff happens.'

Just then, Mum shouts up the stairs.

'Have you heard the news?' she calls.

'What news?'

'It's Kevin Keegan. He's resigned as England manager.'

In stereo, we say:

'Stuff happens.'

2

I'm making my way home from Chloe's house. Her mum and dad asked me over for tea. Bobby laughed his socks off when I told him.

'You're too young for all that malarkey,' he said. 'At our age, girls are for fun. Save all that commitment stuff for when you're over the hill. When you're thirty, or something.'

Funnily enough, tea at Chloe's wasn't as painful as you might think. They were even watching the Derby–Liverpool game when I arrived. Thinking about it, I was the only one who showed much interest in it. Chloe probably got her parents to have it on. She's thoughtful like that. I have to admit to feeling a pinch of guilt. She's so thoughtful, so nice she makes me want to kick myself. How come I find her niceness so irritating? How come I don't feel more strongly about her? I'm fond of her, I really am. But is 'fond' enough? I've tried to make the feelings grow, but it isn't like cultivating a yucca. Some things you can water and water, and they still stay the same size. Even while we were sitting together on the settee, Julie was there, like Banquo's ghost. (In case you're wondering, we've just done *Macbeth*. I thought killing the old king was sick. Bobby thought it was a cool career move. Seems we're as far apart in our views on politics as we are in our attitudes to women. Unbelievably, he's still managing to string Caitlin and Rosie along. Frailty, thy name is Bobby. And yes, I do know that isn't from *Macbeth*.)

I jog across the road by the police station and walk towards the Fusillier. I'm passing the library when I hear familiar laughter. It's Julie. I'd know her voice anywhere. It's always with me. For a moment, I think she's alone. Then I see him.

Fitz.

He unfastens his jacket and drapes it over her shoulders. Thinks he's gallantry personified, that one! Julie glances back at him and smiles. I find myself retreating into the darkness and watching them. I can feel the green monster clawing its way up my throat.

Fitz slips his arms round her waist from behind and she leans back against him. They look comfortable together. Disgust fills me like cold jelly. He's animated, skittish. He's obviously full of Liverpool's 4–0 thrashing of the Rams. United won too this weekend, but Liverpool's victory this afternoon has taken some of the gloss off our win at Leicester. The old enemy are tucked in just behind us in fourth place.

The old enemy. There's only one enemy in my life just now, and that's Fitz. He's got the girl. My girl. He's also got my place in the Year 11 team. I haven't played once this season. No, it's all Fitz. He's the star man. He can't put a foot wrong. I start planning horrible deaths. Just when I'm imagining him choking on a shredded Liverpool scarf, I see him lean forward and nuzzle Julie's cheek. His hands start to move up over her stomach, but she stops him with a playful slap.

'Oh no, you don't,' she says, but her tone of voice is too gentle for my liking. The least he deserved was a slap across the face.

I see her bus coming. She disengages herself from his embrace. She gives him a quick peck as it pulls up at the stop, but he wants more. He presses his lips against hers. I can feel my nails digging into my palms. I could do him some serious damage. Just give me the opportunity. Julie finally draws away from him and gets on the bus. She gives him a wave and starts to move down the bus. Fitz stands there for a couple of minutes like a cat that's had the canary. He sets off home with a spring in his step. I walk away with a heavy tread.

Bobby's struggling to keep up. It's on account of the day I've had. For starters, I was woken by Mum hammering on the bedroom door.

'How many times?' she yells.

'How many times what?'

'How many times have I told you?'

'How many times have you told me *what*?'

I wasn't trying to be funny. I just didn't know what she was on about.

'Leaving loose change in your pockets, that's what! A ten pence piece is jamming the pipe in the washing machine. You've blocked it again. The stupid thing won't drain.'

So what do I say in reply?

'Didn't you check my trousers before you put them in?'

It was just about the worst thing I could have come up with.

'*Me* check them! Terry, you're fifteen, not five. I expect you to check them yourself.'

That was bad enough, but worse was to follow. After that dose of earache from Mum, I was so fed up, I left home without my English coursework. That meant a fifteen minute detention from Spotty. Then, living up to the old saying that disasters come in threes, Six Guns told us about the new PE timetable. We're going to get a lesson a week at the fitness suite at the sports centre, the one Dad goes to.

'What's wrong with that?' Bobby asked. 'It's a gym. A gym, Terry! Where else do you get to watch women sweat?'

'That's the point,' I reminded him. 'Julie will be there, but so will Fitz, rubbing my nose in it. I get to see the pair of them sweat.'

Bobby gave me a sideways look.

'And this is the man who's only got eyes for Chloe Blackburn!'

That last little jibe put me in a nark I still haven't got out of. So here I am, storming down the street with Bobby panting along behind.

118

'Are you sure your old man won't mind us landing on him like this?'

'I don't care if he minds or not,' I tell him. 'I'm not missing the Champions' League, but I'm not staying in the house with *her*.'

Her is Mum. Not satisfied with having a go at me over the washing machine at breakfast time, she met me at the door tonight with a bag of washing.

'I got this out of your room,' she said.

'You went in my room!' I cried, all indignant. 'It's private.'

'It's a tip,' snapped Mum. 'Can't you put anything in the laundry basket?'

So what did I say?

'Oh, get a life, Mum. Dad has. I've met his new girlfriend. She doesn't go on about the laundry, and she doesn't have to OD on Hobnobs, either.'

I could have bitten my tongue off for saying it, but I soon stopped feeling sorry for her. Mum immediately launched into this mega-rant about disgusting teenage boys. I shouted back, and before you know it, there was civil war in the Payne household. So here I am, on my way to Dad's flat to watch United play PSV Eindhoven. I ask you, there's qualification to the second stage hanging in the balance, and Mum gives me aggravation over a few pairs of socks!

'Think your dad'll have anything to eat?' asks Bobby.

'Why, haven't you had anything?'

'No, Slughead's round ours.'

So that's why Bobby turned up on the doorstep. He's been turfed out by Cocker Spaniel Man and he needs somewhere to go.

'You need to eat properly,' I tell him.

Bobby shakes his head: 'Percentage of men who plan their meals: 25. Percentage of women who plan their meals: 90. It's in my genes not to eat properly.'

We ring the bell and Dad answers.

'Oh, Terry.'

'Yes,' I say. 'Terry. Your son, remember. I need a favour. I've had a row with Mum. Can I watch the match here?'

Dad hesitates, so I put on my best hangdog expression.

119

'Yes sure, why not?'

I'm settling down to watch the build-up when I hear water running.

'Cutting it fine, aren't you?' I ask, 'Do you think you've got time for a shower before kick-off?'

Dad's face goes as red as a United shirt.

'It isn't my shower.'

'So who . . . ? Oh.'

Bobby gives a frown of incomprehension, then goes wide-eyed.

'Oh, Muriel.'

Which is the cue for her entrance. She pads in wearing a white towelling robe just as Terry Venables is predicting a narrow United victory.

'Oh, hello lads,' she says. 'Geoff didn't tell me we had company.'

'We're not company,' I tell her. 'I'm family and he's . . .'

I'm not sure quite how to introduce Bobby.

'He's an Evertonian.'

To my horror, Muriel responds with this amazing donkey bray.

Hurrgh-aw, hurrgh-aw, hurrgh-aw.

Muriel! Mule is more like it.

The moment she leaves the room to get changed, Bobby winks.

'Didn't she make an ass of herself?'

Dad smiles thinly.

'That's her only drawback,' he says. 'The laugh from hell.'

But it's kick-off time, so who cares?'

Wednesday 18th October
9.16 p.m.

'No!' I cry, holding my head. *'No!'*

Van Bommel's just equalised for PSV. We could be out of the Champions' League. We were 1–0 up after eight minutes through Teddy Sheringham's header, and flying. Now we could be on our way out of the competition.

'Come on!' I yell as play restarts. 'You can't just throw it away.'

'Takes his football seriously, doesn't he?' says Mule.

She follows up with a manic bray: Hurrgh-aw, hurrgh-aw, hurrgh-aw.

Me and Dad give her daggers simultaneously. There are some things you don't joke about. Suddenly, United have shaken themselves out of their torpor. They're pouring forward. After six minutes, Paul Scholes bursts through, flicking the ball in the air before slamming it home. Barely five minutes later, Dwight Yorke streaks clear of his marker to score our third.

'Yaaarrgh!'

Dad and I are leaping all round the room. Bobby's polishing off the butterscotch ice cream.

'What a terrible noise,' says Mule, wincing at our celebrations.

Me, Dad and Bobby exchange glances then roar with laughter.

Mule looks confused.

Friday 20th October
6.00 p.m.

Chloe has her uses. She's just brokered a peace summit between me and Mum.

'Sorry I blew my top,' says Mum.

'Sorry I mentioned *her*. Mum, she's not a patch on you.'

There's only one way to seal the peace treaty.

'Friday night sugar hunt?' I suggest.

Chloe looks puzzled.

'House tradition,' I explain. 'At the end of the week, we forget diets and dental hygiene and stuff ourselves with sweets. You game?'

Chloe laughs.

'Just you try and stop me.'

So we set off for the offie. It's a Caramel for Mum, Maltesers for Amy, a Flake for Chloe and a Mars bar for me.

'We'll need that lesson at the fitness suite after this,' says Chloe, linking arms with me.

Well, gee thanks for reminding me. My mind flashes to Julie and Fitz.

'Something wrong?' asks Chloe.

'No, why?'

'You went all serious.'

'Just thinking about the game against Leeds tomorrow,' I say, lying through my teeth. 'I'm getting psyched up for it.'

'You and your football,' says Chloe.

I think of Julie and Fitz cheering on Liverpool against Leicester.

'Yes, me and my football.'

Friday 20th October
10.30 p.m.

When I get in from Chloe's, Amy is already tucked up in bed. Mum's in the living room.

'What're you watching?'

'I don't know.'

I look at the TV screen.

'So what've you got it on for?'

'Background noise.'

'Why?'

Mum looks up. For the first time I realise she's been crying.

'Are you OK?'

'Not really, no.'

I give her a questioning look. Even as I'm inviting her to explain, I'm half-wishing she wouldn't.

'I'm lonely, Terry.'

'But you've got us. Me, Amy . . .'

She smiles.

'I know, and you're great kids. But I need more, I need . . .'

'Dad?'

She closes her eyes for a moment.

'I thought I did. Did you know he's the only lad I've ever been out with?'

'You're kidding!'

Which is rich coming from me.

'It's the God's honest truth. Until this summer I never even

thought about our marriage. It was just there. Now . . . Oh, I
don't know what to think.'

'But you'd have him back?'

'I think so.'

Only *think* so!

'You would, wouldn't you?'

'Terry, this other woman, I don't know any more. Nobody
wants to be second best.'

'You're not!'

Mum shakes her head.

'Tell your dad that. He wants her, this Muriel.'

She gets up and walks towards the door. The way she does it
tells me she doesn't want me to follow.

'He certainly doesn't want me.'

Saturday 21st October
1.40 p.m.

'So,' Chloe asks, hands on hips, 'Can we go out *now*?'

'I just want to hear what Fergie's got to say,' I say, waving
her away like a troublesome fly.

I ignore her snort of indignation and strain to catch the great
man's words.

'This is stupid,' says Chloe. 'You've seen the match. Isn't that
enough for you?'

'No,' I tell her. 'A big match is an event. Build-up, game,
inquest. If you're a footy fan, you buy into the whole package.
It's the pattern of life.'

Chloe shakes her head. I don't know why she's so put out. If
United–Leeds hadn't been an 11.30 a.m. kick-off, she would
never have got me to town. As it is, I'm making a big sacrifice.
I'm giving up an afternoon of willing Arsenal, Newcastle and
Liverpool – especially Liverpool – to lose.

'*Now* are we ready?' she asks.

I drag myself away from the TV. When you beat Leeds 3–0
you want to milk every glorious moment.

'Are you off?' calls Mum.

'Yes, just going.'

'Have fun.'

Chloe winks.

'We will.'

She will. I can't believe I agreed to this. We're going shopping. That's right – shopping! Chloe wants a new pair of jeans, and she expects me to stand like a lemon while she tries on a zillion pairs. I know what it's all about, of course. It's this couple thing. She wants us to traipse round Liverpool proclaiming: 'Look at us, we're an item.' All of a sudden, I'm finding loads of little faults with Chloe: the pinched face, the freckled nose, the reedy voice.

Why can't she be . . . why can't she be Julie?

We're waiting at the station when I hear familiar voices. I look up and see a blur of red and gold on the pedestrian bridge. Julie and Fitz, Kelly and Gary. They stand talking just along the platform. It's like they haven't seen us, but I know Fitz has. Suddenly he's talking loudly. I know it's for my benefit.

'Leicester, we'll sweep them aside. Move over, Mancs, now it's our turn.'

I lean forward, stealing a look at Julie. She looks dazzling in her Liverpool away shirt. I'm vaguely aware of Chloe rattling away in my left ear. She's just asked me a question.

'Yes,' I answer.

'Yes!?'

The tone of Chloe's voice tell me I've said the wrong thing.

'I mean no.'

'Are you listening to me, Terry?' she asks.

She spots Julie and gives me a lethal stare. I think she's always had an inkling how I feel. It's the cue for Fitz to come over.

'Well, if it isn't Terry and Chloe,' he says, heavy on the final syllable.

I'm squirming. He's got something on me and he'll have no qualms about using it.

'Got yourself a catch there, Chloe,' he says.

Gary and Kelly laugh appreciatively.

'Oh, clear off, Fitz,' says Chloe.

'Keep your wig on, girl,' says Fitz.

The train pulls up.

'One piece of advice, though,' he says as he boards. 'Keep an eye on Terry here. I hear he's a bit of a lad.'

'What was all that about?' asks Chloe.

'Ignore him,' I tell her. 'He's just trying to wind us up.'

Trying, and succeeding. All the way to Lime Street it's 'Trust matters,' and, 'I couldn't stand it if you turned out like Bobby,' and, 'There definitely isn't anything you want to tell me?'

No, Chloe, there's *nothing* I want to tell you.

For the next two centuries I trail round the shops after Chloe. Between shops, I clock the latest scores. It's bad news: West Ham 1 Arsenal 2; Liverpool 1 Leicester 0. Arsenal are breathing down our necks with Liverpool neatly poised in third place.

'Haven't you made your mind up yet?' I complain.

'I think so,' says Chloe. 'I'm going back to that first shop.'

'The first shop!' I groan. 'So why didn't you get them right away and save us all this wandering round?'

'You don't understand women, do you?' she asks.

I think of Julie snuggled up to Fitz and shake my head.

'No, not one bit.'

Tuesday 24th October
7.45 p.m.

I hear the doorbell ring and close my eyes, willing it to be for Mum or Amy. Not Chloe, please not Chloe.

'Oh, hello Chloe love,' says Mum.

The girl's timing is impeccable. She manages to arrive just as the United–Anderlecht match kicks off in Belgium.

'Oh, not football *again*,' groans Chloe. 'But it's Tuesday night.'

'Champions' League,' I explain. 'If we win tonight, we qualify for the next stage.'

'I see,' says Chloe who clearly doesn't.

So there she sits at the kitchen table while I listen to the game on the radio. I don't know anybody with On-digital so this is the best I can do. I've been looking forward to the match all day, but it doesn't go according to plan. For starters, there's

Chloe with a face like a smacked bottom. Then there's the little matter of the score.

Anderlecht 1, Man. United 0. Despair.

Anderlecht 2, Man. United 0. Disbelief.

Anderlecht 2, Man. United 1. Relief.

Dennis Irwin's penalty just before half-time is a glimmer of hope.

'How much longer?' asks Chloe, bringing me a Coke.

'Forty-five minutes. You know, the second half.'

That face again. A pinched bottom.

'Look Chloe,' I say, 'You don't have to stay.'

'Is that it?' she says. 'Do you want me to go?'

Say yes, you dope. You know this isn't working. Be brave for once.

'No, of course I don't want you to go.'

Coward!

'I just mean, you look bored.'

'I *am* bored, Terry. It's a wonder that stupid Bobby isn't here too.'

'No, he's out with Rosie. Or is it Caitlin?'

I pick up the *Mirror* and start scribbling on a piece of scrap paper.

'Now what are you doing?'

'Adjusting the Group G table to see how we stand if the score stays the same.'

'Terry,' she says, 'That is so . . . *sad.*'

I ignore her. The teams are out for the second half. In the opening exchanges, it's all United. But is the damage already done? Have our defensive frailties in the first half cost us the match? We're on top, all right, but no breakthrough.

'I don't believe it,' I murmur, with a quarter of an hour left. 'We're not going to make it.'

I catch Chloe's eye. Maybe she's thinking the same about us.

Fergie throws on Solskjaer for Irwin, an attacker for a defender.

'He's going for it,' I hiss.

But Anderlecht hold out. I slump against the freezer in despair. There is only one flicker of hope on a bleak evening.

At least PSV Eindhoven have been held to a draw in Kiev. That means we hold on to second place in the group.

'Can I talk now?' asks Chloe.

'Sure,' I say, reaching to switch off the radio.

That's when everything falls apart. The presenter announces a correction. PSV have *won* in Kiev. That puts us third and on course for elimination. I bury my face in my hands. Belgian suicide.

'Oh, grow up, Terry,' says Chloe. 'It's only a game.'

'Do you ever think before you open that stupid mouth?' I snap.

Chloe's face drains of colour. Moments later, she bursts into tears. Let it go, I tell myself. Remember what Bobby says: sometimes you've got to be cruel to be kind. This relationship isn't working. So do us both a favour and do nothing.

'Terry, I didn't think you could be like this.'

Instinctively, I offer her a hankie. She shrugs my hand away. Don't do it. Remember, cruel to be kind. But I ignore my inner voice.

'Go on, take it.'

Then, the fateful words:

'I was upset about the match. I didn't mean it. Honest.'

You did mean it, Terry Payne, and you're not being honest. Chloe takes the hankie and gives me a thin smile, like she's reminding herself she likes me. I can't stand seeing her miserable, so I do the nice thing, the coward's thing. As if trying to prove I don't understand her, or myself, I do the only thing I ever do when we hit a crisis.

I kiss her.

3

'This is agony,' I whisper.

'Are you feeling all right?' asks Bobby.

No, Bobby, I'm not feeling all right. The cause of my agony is Julie. She's right there in front of me, just a heartbeat away. Bobby and I are on the row of cross-trainers behind her, pushing pedals, pulling handles. Julie and Fitz are side by side on the treadmills, pounding the track in unison. That's right, it's the first of 11S's sessions at the fitness suite.

And it really is agony.

I don't mean the exercise, either. The wall in front of us is mirrored, so here I am looking at the girl of my dreams from two angles at once. Julie Carter is jogging. No, whatever she's doing, you couldn't call it jogging. She's running hard, taking long, athletic strides. But it seems effortless. Her feet hardly seem to touch the treadmill. She's hovering, that's what she's doing, hovering over the moving track, her arms moving as gracefully as featherless wings. I've tried not to look at her, but there isn't a thing I can do about it. My eyes have taken on a life of their own. They're drawn to every movement of her body in her black and violet body-suit, every flick of her plaited, coal-black hair. She's an eye-magnet. But here's the reason for my agony. She's not my girl. She's with Fitz. And doesn't he want to rub it in! Every time I steal the slightest glance at her, he's flashing a knowing look my way, as if to say:

Dream on, loser. The girl is mine.

But still I look, and every time I look his eyes meet mine.

The girl is mine.

128

Julie seems totally unaware of my interest, but she must have noticed. All I want is a glance, the ghost of a smile, anything to say there is something between us.

What am I saying?

She's got her boyfriend right there beside her and here I am, Dufus of the Century, willing her to give me the come-on. As if the humiliating presence of Fitz isn't enough, Chloe will be back any minute. Her group is getting the guided tour. Small weights room, aerobic suite, spa bath, sauna, steam room.

'Nice bum,' says Bobby, just a little bit too loud.

Fitz glances round, not at Bobby but at me. And he's grinning. Like a cat that's licked the cream.

Nice bum, his eyes are telling me. *Too right.*

And it's mine.

She's mine.

Which has me dreaming up The World's Most Appalling Gym Accidents:

Promising footballer shredded in treadmill horror.

Teenager sucked into extractor fan. Bloodstains found as far as Huyton.

GCSE student strangled in gym. Over-long trainer laces to blame.

But nothing can touch Frisky Fitzy. The boy's fireproof. The Teflon kid, that's him.

I'm still scraping the gore from my imagination when Chloe returns. She gives a little frown when she sees how close I am to Julie.

'Nearly done?' she asks, a definite coolness in her voice.

'Yes,' I say. 'I'm going for a shower.'

'Cold one?' asks Bobby.

The joke goes down like a lead balloon. As Chloe stamps towards the female changing rooms, I give Bobby daggers.

'What?' he asks, all innocent.

I push past him and take a shallow breath. It's been a tough hour.

Like I said earlier:

Agony.

Fitz and Gary Tudor have taken over the changing rooms. They're laughing like hyenas and flicking each other with towels. I find myself scowling.

'What's up with you?' asks Fitz, spotting the look on my face.

'Nothing that couldn't be put right by you falling down a lift shaft,' I tell him, flushing beetroot at being rumbled.

Fitz smirks.

'Watching the match tonight?' he asks.

'Yes, what of it?'

'I hope you get stuffed,' he says. 'I hope Kiev put five past you.'

He's touched a raw nerve. United need to win to qualify for the next stage of the Champions' League. We've thrown it away before. Against Gothenberg, Monaco, Borussia Dortmund. I couldn't stand another disappointment.

'I can't see that happening,' says Gary Tudor. 'But Kiev might get a draw. If that happens, the Mancs still go out.'

'Dream on,' I say, trying to sound more confident than I feel.

They give these big, forced laughs and head for the showers.

'You're going out, Manc,' they chorus. 'Ki-ev, Ki-ev.'

'Ignore them,' says Bobby. 'What's the difference between a Liverpool fan and a kettle?'

'Don't know.'

'A kettle can sing.'

Bobby makes me feel better, but not for long. A couple of minutes later, Fitz and Gary are back. Fitz is showing off a photograph and looking round at me.

'Let's have a butcher's,' says Gary.

Paul Scully and Jamie Seddon join the huddle. Scully gives a low whistle.

'Lucky dog,' he says.

'Show the Manc,' says Gary. 'Let him know what he's missing.'

Fitz flashes the photo. It's of Fitz and Julie. I knew they went to a Hallowe'en party a week last Sunday, but I'd never seen their costumes. In the pic, Fitz is dressed as an executioner. As for Julie, she's . . .

She's . . .

Ohmigod, she's stunning!

She's wearing a red miniskirt and top, red tights and shoes and little red horns. My angel, dressed as a gorgeous devil.

'Put it away,' I tell him.

'Got any of Chloe?' asks Gary. 'What did she go as?'

'Stick insect,' says Fitz.

'No, with that hair and that figure she could pass for a matchstick,' says Scully.

'Get stuffed!'

'Oo-ooh!'

'Poor old Terry,' says Fitz. 'Stuck with the wrong girl and about to get booted out of Europe.'

'At least we're in Europe,' I retort.

I'm acutely aware that I'm not defending Chloe, and I feel terrible.

'What about you? Beaten by Leeds and struggling to qualify in the UEFA Cup against some Czech no-hopers.'

Fitz shakes his head.

'And what about the great Michael Owen?' I ask, following him to the changing room doors.

'He's injured,' says Fitz. 'He had to have a brain scan after a head injury.'

'Two,' I say, correcting him.

We're out in the foyer.

'What?'

'Owen had two brain scans,' I tell him. 'And do you know why?'

'No, but I'm sure you're going to tell me.'

'Because they couldn't find his brain the first time.'

I'm warming to my theme.

'Let's face it, he isn't the sharpest blade of grass in the lawn. I bet there are cauliflowers with a bigger IQ. That's right, he's got the intelligence of a brussels sprout!'

For some reason, Fitz is grinning. I turn round and my heart turns to blancmange. Julie's looking right at me. There's me having a whale of a time slagging off her hero, and she's been listening the whole way through. That's one thing I have to say for myself. My timing is brilliant . . .

. . . Just brilliant!

Wednesday 8th November
7.45 p.m.

I'm watching the match at home.

Alone.

Dad's gone out for a meal with Mule. Mum's taken Amy to a friend's birthday party. Bobby's gone out with Caitlin. Or is it Rosie? Either way, all I've got for company is a can of Red Bull and a packet of Monster Munch.

'Come on, lads. Bury them.'

I can just hear Fitz if we fail to win.

'Ki-ev! Ki-ev!'

These Ukrainians have just become honorary Scousers.

We start brightly, taking the game to them. The first fifteen minutes are played completely in their half. Giggsy's running the show, turning their defence inside out with his mazy runs. But with a quarter of an hour gone, we still haven't scored. I'm getting anxious.

'Come on!'

After eighteen minutes United turn up the heat. Sheringham clears out of defence, the ball bounces around the penalty area for a few seconds and Teddy's on hand to stab it home.

'Sher-in-gham!'

Take that, Fitzy. We'll bury them now.

Only we don't. Just before half-time, Giggsy limps off with a hamstring injury. From then on, it's cat-on-hot-bricks-time. Mum and Amy come in just after half-time. I'm on the edge of the sofa, willing United to keep them out.

'You're winning then?' says Mum.

'Yes, 1–0, but we're making life difficult for ourselves.'

'Best leave him,' Mum tells Amy. 'Football.'

Amy nods.

Football.

We've lost momentum and Kiev are attacking. Barthez has had nothing to do in goal, but at 1–0 you're always vulnerable.

132

'Come on!'

Just a couple of minutes to go.

'We're going to do it.'

'Terry,' calls Mum.

'What!'

'It's Chloe.'

'Not now.'

'Aren't you going to speak to the girl?'

'Not . . . now!'

'But . . .'

'Tell her I'll phone her back.'

'OK.'

Mum's voice is disapproving. I don't care. Bodnar's just crossed low from the right. The substitute Demetradze sprints through to meet it. For a moment the world stands still. It's easier to score than to miss.

A draw and we're out.

'No-o-o . . .'

Demetradze shoots in slow motion.

'. . . o-o-o . . .'

He misses.

'Yiss! You camel, you great big Ukrainian camel!'

Three minutes of extra time.

'What? Where did you get three minutes from ref?'

But we hold firm. We're through. Take that, Fitz. I live to fight another day.

'Are you going to phone Chloe back?' asks Mum.

'Can't I just hear what Fergie has to say first?'

'Please.'

'OK.'

I dial Chloe's number.

'Yes?'

It's her. Her voice is flat.

'Sorry I couldn't come to the phone. It was a big moment in the match.'

'You never have time for me,' says Chloe.

A moment's pause, then the killer.

'I saw how you were looking at Julie.'

'I never! I wasn't!'

133

Truly, I protest too much.

'When you've made your mind up what you want,' says Chloe, 'tell me.'

Time for courage, Terry lad. End it now.

'Just be honest, Terry. What do you want?'

As usual, my courage fails. I just can't stand the disappointment in her voice.

'I want you, Chloe. You.'

'See you tomorrow, then.'

'Yes, tomorrow.'

I put the phone down and walk back into the living room. They're rerunning the Sheringham goal. My heart is full. Unfortunately, it's not on account of Chloe.

4

So this is how it stands. With a month to go until the United v.
Liverpool game and five weeks until Christmas, life is really
starting to suck. In fact, this winter is turning out to be the
suckingest season that ever sucked. I've got a girl, but she's not
the girl. When I'm out with Chloe all I can see is Julie, Julie and
Fitz. Fitz with his Michael Owen haircut and his Liverpool
shirt.

Which makes me feel guilty.

Which makes me feel bad.

As if that wasn't enough, my parents are getting divorced.
Yes, the paperwork has finally started to go through. Mum left
the envelope on the kitchen table this morning. Some family!
Dad's going out with this old slapper with her bottled tan and
her laugh like a jackass, and Mum's eating for England.

The Hobnob champion of Prescot.

Which makes me feel guilty.

Which makes me . . . Well, you get the message.

I mean, what happened to happy? Just a few months ago I
was a season ticket-holder with a full set of parents and an
unbroken heart. You know what, you ought to be able to live
your life over twice, once as a rehearsal and the second time
for real. Wouldn't that be brilliant? Looking back, I can see
where it all went wrong.

So I just rerun my life to one Saturday in June. I'm on my
doorstep and Julie's got her liquid brown eyes trained on me. I
untie my tongue and say the words that could change my life:
'Would you like to do something tomorrow?'

But life's a single take. You only get one go at it. Typical. I throw myself back on the bed and stare at the ceiling. Chloe's gone to her nan's and Bobby's out with Caitlin. Or is it Rosie? Anyway, I'm all on my lonesome.

An REM song drifts up from the living room. 'Everybody hurts.' We're soulmates, me and Mum. Two human beings twenty-one years apart, but only a packet of Hobnobs between us. A few minutes later she's playing: 'Losing my religion.'

At least I've got that. United: the one true religion, the once and future champions. We play City tomorrow at Maine Road, the first derby match in four years. My mind dredges up a date. 23rd September, 1989. Manchester City 5, Manchester United 1. I was only four when it happened, but my skin still burns with humiliation at the thought of it. We've a score to settle tomorrow. A thumping victory might take my mind off Julie and me.

Might.

Saturday 18th November
11.20 a.m.

I'm at my Dad's. I've got Bobby in tow. Caitlin's gone to town with her mates and Rosie is away seeing family. So Man City v. Man Utd on Sky gets the nod. While the old man is making toasted sausage butties for in-match sustenance, we inspect the living room for signs of Mule. Nothing, not a lipstick, not a hairbrush, not a nail varnish. The whole place has had Mule-ectomy. Bobby raises an eyebrow.

'You don't think . . . ?'

'Beats me. To be honest, I'm past caring.'

It's not true, but it has a finality about it. It helps keep Bobby off the subject of the divorce.

'Hey,' says Bobby. 'I didn't tell you, did I? Fitz and Julie have had a tiff.'

My heart skips a beat.

'Of course, you won't want to know.'

His eyes twinkle with mischief.

'You're so loyal to Chloe.'

I scowl.

'Let's have the details, Bobby. Cough.'

'Caitlin told me. They were waving their arms about and shouting at each other.'

'Any idea what it was about?'

Bobby gives a shake of his head.

' 'Fraid not, but maybe, just maybe, all isn't well in paradise.'

I think of Julie and feel hope. I think of Chloe and feel guilt. Maybe . . .

. . . just maybe.

Dad comes in carrying a tray. Toasted sausage sarnies, two cans of Coke, a mug of tea.

'Tea man, are you Geoff?' says Bobby.

'Yes, coffee's too bitter.'

'But you don't know which country is the world's number one tea drinker.'

'No, I don't, but I'm sure you're going to tell me.'

'Irish Republic. One thousand, four hundred and twelve cups per person per year. It just pushes the UK into second place.'

'Well, fancy that.'

Dad delivers the line in a bored monotone. Something's up. I think about Mule's laugh and the absence of her stuff and wonder.

Maybe . . .

. . . just maybe.

Imagine. What if it all came together? Fitz splits with Julie. Dad dumps Mule. Me and Julie, Mum and Dad, the order of the universe restored. Send me a sign, oh gods of football. A win for United to tell me everything is going to be all right with the world, after all.

Saturday 18th November
11.32 a.m.

'Goalllllll!'

David Beckham shoots from thirty-five yards. The shot travels at 68.2 miles per hour. Unsighted, Nicky Weaver in the Manchester City goal takes a step to the left. In an instant the ball has sailed past his flailing arms into the net.

'A sign from the gods,' I murmur.
'What's that?' asks Bobby.
'Oh nothing.'

Saturday 18th November
2.00 p.m.

Mum greets me at the door.
'Good, your're back. Oh, hi Bobby.'
'Hi, Sharon.'
'I've got to nip out to the shops,' says Mum. 'Would you stay in with Amy?'
'Sure.'
'How did United get on?'
'Won 1–0.'
'Well, that'll make half of Manchester happy.'
Bobby immediately heads for the kitchen.
'Sorry Bobby,' says Mum. 'I didn't buy any biscuits, so you're out of luck.'
'Cakes?'
'No sweet stuff of any description.'
Bobby and I exchange glances.
'You mean . . .'
'That's right,' says Mum. 'I've made up my mind. Look out world, I'm getting into shape.'
I give silent thanks to the gods of football. Today's victory is an omen. I can see it all. Dad dumps Mule. Mum loses weight. Dad comes back to Mum. Julie dumps Fitz. I ask her out. Clouds of apple blossom shower us as we walk into the sunset. Life has a purpose after all.
Maybe . . .
. . . just maybe.

Sunday 19th November
4.00 p.m.

I'm at Chloe's house.
I know, I know. Here I am thinking almost non-stop about Julie and whether she's broken up with Fitz, and at the same

time I'm sitting on Chloe's settee, holding Chloe's hand and watching Chloe's television. I guess that makes me a pretty lousy human being. Well, I'm not proud of what I'm doing. I admit it. I'm a coward, a bona fide, yellow through and through coward.

(But at least Chloe's got Sky Sports 1).

And having Sky Sports 1 is a real bonus, because – guess what – the gods of football have continued to smile on me. Get this, not only did United win yesterday but all the obvious challengers lost. That's right, Arsenal, Leeds and Aston Villa all got beaten. I've convinced myself that everything's going my way. Which makes my behaviour stringing Chloe along even more disgusting. But I continue to play the game.

The conversation goes something like this:

Chloe: 'So why are you watching this match?'

Me: 'Liverpool are playing. They're one of United's main rivals for the title.'

Chloe: 'So you're supporting Tottenham?'

Me: 'Yes.'

Chloe: 'And you like them?'

Me: 'No. I *hate* them.'

Chloe: 'I don't think I'll ever get the hang of this.'

Ten minutes into the match she's got her head on my shoulder. For crying out loud, you don't cuddle during football! She really hasn't got the hang of it. The conversation resumes:

Chloe: 'Terry, can I ask you something?'

Me (thinking): 'No!'

Me (speaking): 'Go on.'

Chloe: 'Have you got feelings for Julie Carter?'

Me (thinking): 'Not half.'

Luckily, I don't have to answer her. At that very moment Robbie Fowler scores for Liverpool.

Me (relieved at the let-off, but sickened by the scoreline): 'Look at that! The Tottenham defence just went AWOL.'

I sit there uncomfortably, knowing she's bound to bring up the subject of Julie again. Gods of football, why have you forsaken me? Chloe's about to ask again when they finally smile once more. Ferdinand equalises for Spurs. Two minutes later I go on a turbo-driven celebration. Sherwood has put the Londoners in the lead. At full-time Liverpool have gone down to a 2–1 defeat. It's been a weekend to remember.

'Happy now?' asks Chloe.

I count my blessings. United five points clear at the top of the Premiership; Julie and Fitz quarrelling; the Dad–Mule thing cooling; Mum kicking out the Hobnobs. Happy? I'm delirious. It's just too good to be true.

Monday 21st November
9.00 a.m.

It *was* too good to be true. I should have known as much when I left home with Travis' 'Why does it always rain on me?' ringing in my ears. The moment I got to the end of the street it lashed it down. By the time I got to the school gates I was soaked to my undies.

I phoned Dad last night. He was on his way out – you've guessed it – with Mule. They haven't split up after all. Then I caught Mum opening her secret Hobnob stash. Diet, my eye! But that isn't the worst of it. I've just seen Julie and Fitz. She looked lovely with raindrops sparkling on her eyelashes. Then she went and spoiled the effect by going up to Fitz and giving him a peck on the cheek. Nothing passionate, you understand, but enough to tell me they haven't broken up.

Gods of football?

Who am I kidding?

5

Why do I bother?

I mean, why do I rotten well bother?

As usual, I've run all the way to Amy's school to pick her up and dragged her all the way back, protesting at the top of her whiny, little voice, just so I can get a game for the Year 11 team.

But do I play? Do I heck!

Six Guns thinks the sun shines out of Fitz. He's always first on the team sheet. Captain, playmaker, top scorer. No rotation here. Week in, week out yours truly sits kicking his heels on the subs' bench. I haven't started a single game this term. My only appearance has been five minutes taking Paul Scully's place when he got an elbow in the face. It wasn't even enough time to get my shorts mucky.

Amy doesn't help either.

'Why do you keep coming?' she asks. 'They never pick you.'

'I'll get my chance,' I growl, burying my face in my tracksuit top.

'When?'

Yes, when? I'm way down Six Gun's pecking order. That's me all right, lower than birdseed.

'Lucky last night, weren't you?' Fitz asks as he leads the team out.

'Lucky?' I snort. 'We won 3–1.'

Against Panathanaikos, that is, the Greek champions. Second phase of the Champions' League.

141

'Oh, you won all right. But if they'd taken half their chances you'd have got battered.'

I stare after him. Why didn't I taunt him about Liverpool losing at Spurs? Why didn't I remind him they're nine points behind us in the Premiership? Why didn't I say *something*?

I'll tell you why. Because he's with Julie and that means he'll always get one over on me.

Bobby comes over and sits next to me. He isn't even a sub this evening. Six Guns says he's out of condition. Putting on the beef is the way he puts it.

'Noticed anything?' Bobby asks.

'No.'

'Look around you.'

I look. The penny drops.

'Julie, she isn't here.'

'Got it in one, Sherlock.'

'So where . . . ?'

'That's the million dollar question. Something's going on.'

'But I saw them kissing.'

'And Caitlin's seen them arguing. I tell you, it could be the beginning of the end. Fitzy might just be losing her.'

I feel like yelling out loud, but just then Chloe puts in an appearance. Even though she hates football, she always turns up to support me. Usually that just means watching me sit on the bench. Chloe doesn't mind, though. I grimace with guilt. She's such a heartbreakingly nice person.

'Maybe next time,' she says.

'Yes, next time.'

Maybe . . .

. . . just maybe.

Friday 24th November
8.00 p.m.

Charlie's Angels.

Got that? Charlie's rotten Angels!

I've been dragged along to some lameoid films in my time, but this really takes the biscuit.

'Well, what do you want to see?' asks Chloe.

'It's all right,' I tell her. 'I'm cool.'

I'm buying a couple of tubs of Häagen Dazs, when I feel Chloe squeeze my arm.

'What's up?'

'Seen who's here?'

It's Julie. She looks great. Black leather trousers and a strapless top. I mean, gulp! For a moment I can't see Fitz and my spirits rise. Then I spot him getting the tickets. Lousy mesomorph. He sees me and sarcastically blows a kiss. I want to stuff it back down his stupid throat.

'What does she look like?' says Chloe sourly.

A million dollars, I think. Her mane of glossy black hair is cascading over her bare shoulders.

A fifteen-year-old Cleopatra.

'Dunno,' I say.

Obviously, I'm not convincing Chloe of my disapproval.

'You don't like that sort of thing, do you?' she asks.

Which means: *You don't like* her, *do you?*

I restrict myself to a casually shrugged shoulder, but inside I'm anything but casual. I'm like a can of Coke that's just been shaken within an inch of its fizz.

'You OK?'

'Sure,' I say. 'I'm fine.'

Chloe darts a glare at Julie. I'm not fooling her one bit.

Every now and then in the film theatre I steal a glance at Julie and Fitz. They're sitting five rows in front of us. Chloe catches my eye twice and snuggles up possessively. I squeeze back. What am I doing? Why can't I just be honest and tell her this isn't working? Because I'm a coward, that's why. Yellow right through. If I ever had any bottle, it's gone the way of the ten green ones.

'Is there any Fanta left?' asks Chloe.

I grunt and pass it. Just as I'm handing it over, Julie gets up and runs up the aisle and out of the cinema. Fitz races after her. I follow them with my eyes. I feel like going after them.

'I wonder what that's all about?' says Chloe.

I disguise my interest with another mock-casual shrug, but my mind is working overtime.

Is it the beginning of the end?

Closure.

That's what the Americans call it, closure. I saw it on *Friends*. Tying up the loose ends, putting your mistakes behind you, opening a new chapter in your life. Yes, I really do want closure.

Mum and Dad back together.

Closure.

Me back in the school team.

Closure.

United secure as Premiership champions.

Closure.

Most of all, Julie free of Fitz. Then I can tell Chloe. Gently, but finally.

Closure.

But life isn't like that. Life's open-ended, contradictory, confusing. I haven't got the foggiest idea what my parents are up to. All I get from Mum is: 'It's with the solicitor.' And from Dad, 'it's your mum's move next.' He's keeping tight-lipped about Mule, too. I haven't heard her bray for a few days, but that doesn't mean much. Maybe he's just hiding her away. Suddenly, I can't even rely on United either. Just when things are looking hunky-dory, with the Red Devils eight points clear at the top of the Premiership, disaster strikes. Last night, Fergie fielded a scratch side against Sunderland in the Worthington Cup. It was a practice match, that's all. Or so I thought. But Dwight Yorke goes and gets himself sent off, doesn't he? Now he's going to miss the Liverpool game. That's right, the mother and father of all battles, the grudge match of the season. Andy Cole is already sidelined with an injury so we're down to just two fit senior strikers.

And to cap it all, I'm completely in the dark about Julie and Fitz. Everything tells me their relationship is on the rocks; the rows I've been told about, that walkout at the cinema. But there they are right in front of me on the treadmill, together as if nothing has happened. They're jogging side by side, the beautiful couple, the item. I hate this lesson at the gym. I have to run alongside Chloe, pretending to have eyes only for her, and all the time there's Julie.

Lovely Julie.

Making my heart jump.

Making my flesh crawl with the lies I'm telling Chloe each time we kiss.

So there's no closure.

Only hurt.

Wednesday 29th November
11.45 a.m.

I step out of the shower and right into Fitz's path. I take in the mesomorphic chest and shoulders, the Michael Owen haircut.

'It was criminal, that tackle of Yorke's,' he says. 'Could have finished that player's career.'

'It was mistimed,' I reply. 'Dwight isn't that sort of player.'

'Got your just desserts though, didn't you?' Fitz continues regardless. 'You're out of the Worthington Cup.'

'Fergie was only playing the reserves,' I point out.

'*You're* the reserves,' says Fitz, earning an appreciative chuckle from Gary Tudor. 'How long is it since you played a game?'

I hold my tongue, mainly because I can't think of anything to say.

'What do they say on that quiz programme on telly? Yes, you are the weakest link. Goodbye.'

'Missing link's more like it,' says Gary.

Fitz grins.

'Come to think about it, you are a bit Neanderthal, Terry. Dragging your knuckles on the ground doesn't help you play football, you know.'

'Get lost,' I say, shoving past.

'Come to think of it,' Fitz says. 'I don't know why you bother to turn up at all. Face it, Terry, you'll never get a game with me in your way.'

I think of him playing in place of me.

I think of him holding Julie's hand, kissing her . . .

. . . in place of me . . .

'You are the weakest link.'
. . . holding her . . .
. . . in place of me . . .
'Goodbye.'

6

'Happy birthday, Terry.'

Mum greets me at the bottom of the stairs.

'Thanks.'

'Sixteen, eh? Growing up fast.'

Does she have to do this? I mean, I didn't mind it when I was six. Lapped it up. Wanting to be the big man. It's a bit much at my age. It's a wonder she doesn't pinch my cheeks and tousle my hair!

'My present to you is on the coffee table.'

Change of voice.

'So's your Dad's.'

I see the two identical parcels, slim packages in gold paper. Mum's the one who wrapped them. Obvious. They've got that female neatness about them. I get fifty quid and a CD from each of them. One's Zombie Nation, which must have come from Mum. The other's Victoria Beckham. That definitely came from Dad.

'Thanks, Mum.'

Amy wanders past in her dressing gown and tiger slippers.

'I know what Chloe's got for you.'

'Oh no you don't, young lady,' says Mum, ushering her into the kitchen. 'You're not spoiling the surprise.'

The words are barely out of her mouth when the doorbell rings.

'It's Chloe,' says Mum, twitching the net curtains.

Chloe! At 10.00 a.m. on a Saturday. Doesn't the girl sleep? She'll be cooking breakfast for me next!

147

'Happy birthday,' she says, simultaneously kissing me on the cheek and shoving a parcel into my hands.

'What's this?' I ask.

'Open it.'

Her eyes are sparkling.

'The United away shirt!' I cry. 'Thanks.'

Chloe grabs my hand.

'And . . .'

Inside the shirt I discover the video of: 'United beyond the promised land.'

'I left the receipt in the bag,' says Chloe, 'in case you want to change them.'

'No,' I say, 'Everything's brilliant!'

She's just spend over sixty pounds on me, or her parents have. In the middle of the delight I feel a wave of guilt. This is the girl I'm thinking of dumping.

'You shouldn't have,' I say, my insides twisting with shame. 'It's too much.'

'Not for you, Terry,' she says, giving me a hug. 'Not for you.'

That surge of guilt is becoming a tidal wave.

Saturday 2nd December
3.15 p.m.

Amy lets Dad in. He finds me and Chloe listening to the United–Spurs match on the radio. At least, I'm listening. Chloe's humouring me. She's taking sneaky peaks at her GCSE Revision Guide on the sly. I glanced at it a few minutes ago. She was reading a page called Factorising a Quadratic. Doing a what to a what? I mean, it sounds really painful! It just reminds me how bad I am at maths.

'Happy birthday, son,' says Dad chasing the Factorised Quadratic out of my head.

'Thanks Dad.'

For the present and the chased Quadratic.

He's looking round the kitchen as if he's never been here before. I can't remember the last time he was in the house. Mum hovers in the kitchen doorway, darting accusing looks his way. Dad looks uncomfortable.

'Told our Terry about tonight, Sharon?'

'No, I was waiting for you to arrive.'

'Tonight?' I ask.

'We're going out for a Chinese meal,' says Chloe excitedly.

'We?'

'You and me, Bobby and Caitlin, Amy, your Mum and Dad.'

I stare. Mum . . . and Dad! He senses my shock.

'That's right, the seven of us.'

He changes the subject.

'So who got you the shirt?'

That's right, I'm already wearing it.

'Chloe.'

Dad gives a knowing look. Chloe blushes. Why did she have to go overboard? Why does she have to be so rotten nice?

'So what's the score?' asks Dad.

'0–0.'

'Liverpool?'

'1–0 up.'

Dad scowls.

'There's one bit of good news. Leeds are losing 3–0.'

Dad nods approvingly.

'I see where you get it from,' says Chloe.

'Sorry?'

'Your football mania.'

That's not all I get from him. Imagine if Chloe knew how I've been feeling. She'd be so betrayed. Suddenly the shirt is making my skin burn. I want to feel the same way you do, Chloe, I really want to.

I want to, but I can't. Not towards you, anyway.

'Amy and I are going to the shops, Chloe,' says Mum. 'Want to come and leave the boys to their match?'

Chloe slips on her coat and follows Mum to the door.

'That girl's mad about you,' says Dad.

United are pressing. The comment is *de*pressing.

'I know.'

'What about you?'

What do I say? The truth? That she's OK to be going on

149

with. Until Julie's free. It makes me sound so mercenary. Luckily, Paul Scholes is surging forward, dispensing with the need to reply.

Goooaaallll!

I use the good news from Old Trafford as an excuse to ignore Dad's question. What can I say? What about me?

Saturday 2nd December
9.00 p.m.

I've been in more uncomfortable situations, but I can't remember when. Present around the table at the Chinese Garden are seven people. Of the seven, only one, Amy, is blissfully unaware of the tensions pulsating around us. That's hardly a surprise, of course; she is only nine.

It's all about what those present are trying *not* to do:

Mum and Dad trying not to mention the divorce.

Bobby and Caitlin trying not to mention the Other Girl, who he insists doesn't exist but obviously does.

Me and Chloe trying not to mention Julie.

All that Amy has to avoid saying is that she would have preferred to go to McDonald's. Life's easy when you're nine.

'Well,' says Dad, finishing a half of lager, 'That's another million brain cells killed off.'

'Actually,' says Bobby, gulping down the last of his crispy duck and entering the database of useless facts that is his brain, 'the theory now is that we grow brain cells throughout our lives.'

He goes on to mention something called the hippocampus which sounds like a big university but probably isn't.

'When did you swallow that encyclopaedia, Bobby?' asks Dad.

Detecting the sour note, Chloe dives in the way she has all evening. She is determined to make us all:

a) get along

b) stay cool

c) look happy

Whether we actually *are* happy is irrelevant. Chloe must have been genetically-engineered in Disneyworld. Her consti-

150

tuent parts are ninety-nine per cent niceness and one per cent sweetness.

She brings the perfect presents, laughs at my lamest jokes and does her best to make everybody feel good about themselves. She's got to be the perfect girlfriend. So why on earth do I still think about Julie?

Bobby tries to kick-start the conversation:

'So how's Mu–?'

I kick him under the table.

'Mu– Manchester United? Still winning?'

'Yes, we beat Spurs 2–0.'

A lamer attempt at recovering the situation we couldn't have engineered. Mum's eyes narrow. Dad tugs at his shirt collar. Caitlin gives Bobby daggers. I think she's just been waiting for an excuse. Finally, Chloe gives this high-pitched giggle.

'The last pancake, anybody?'

Pancake.

That about sums up this birthday.

Pancake.

As in as flat as.

Saturday 2nd December
9.45 p.m.

I'm in the Gents' washing my hands when Dad comes in.

'Well,' he sighs, 'It's nearly over.'

'Pretty awful, eh?' I say.

He nods.

'Feel that Arctic wind sweeping in from your Mum?'

'Chloe means well,' I say.

Another nod.

'You and Mum still at war?' I ask.

'That's just it,' he tells me. 'I want to patch things up. I've finished with Mule . . . Muriel.'

My senses swim. This is brilliant.

'No way!'

'You're not going to believe this,' says Dad.

'Try me.'

151

'I'm starting to realise how I feel about your Mum. Maybe comfortable isn't such a bad thing after all. I think I've made a terrible mistake.'

My heart skips a beat.

'Have you told her that?'

'I'm trying.'

Closure, he's talking about closure.

'Then try harder.'

As we return to the table I glance at Chloe. Typical. Here's Dad wondering how to get Mum back, and all the time I'm wondering how to get shot of Chloe.

Doesn't anybody ever get anything right in this world?

7

'Some mistake!' I say, reminding him about Saturday night.

Dad and I are sitting in his shoebox of a living-room with our fish and chips on trays on our knees. We're supposed to be listening to the football phone-in. United play Sturm Graz tomorrow in Austria. But somehow we can't keep our minds on the game. We're thinking about Mum.

'Why couldn't you have worked this out earlier?' I ask.

Dad shrugs.

'I know, I know,' I say, beginning to feel sorry for him. 'I've heard the song. You don't know what you've got till it's gone. What I don't understand is why it's taken you so long? For goodness sake, the divorce is already on its way through. Talk about taking it down to the wire! So why?'

'Dunno,' he says. 'Male vanity, I suppose. When I met Mule . . .'

I burst out laughing.

'When I met *Muriel*, I just couldn't believe she was interested in me. Let's face it, she's a good-looking woman.'

I grimace. I'd rather not face it, thank you very much Dad.

'It had been nearly twenty years since another woman showed an interest in me. It took time, but in the end I realised she wasn't the one.'

He lowered his eyes.

'One simple reason: she wasn't your mum.'

'So you want to walk round Asda in matching pullies after all?'

Dad smiles.

153

'Yes, I suppose I do.'

'And you've told Mum that?'

His expression changes.

'Not in so many words.'

'Then tell her. Tell her tonight.'

Dad frowns.

'I don't know if I can.'

'Why not?'

'Maybe it's a man thing,' says Dad. 'We're all emotionally illiterate. You won't believe this, but when I was your age I was always so tongue-tied with girls. I could never pluck up the courage to talk to them.'

I don't believe what I'm hearing. That's me he's describing.

'Then once, just once, I managed to say what I felt. That's how I got your mum to go out with me.'

He shakes his head.

'The way I see it, finding the right person is a lottery. Once, maybe twice, in your life you come across The One. And you know what, if you don't seize the moment right there and then, you can end up regretting it for the rest of your life.'

There's the sound of a million pennies dropping. Once, maybe twice, in your life! I could be blowing the only chance I'm ever going to get. At sixteen, I could be condemning myself to a lonely bachelorhood! Ohmigod, sixteen years old and I'll never be loved! I've got to tell Julie. It's what Bobby's been telling me all these months. Why didn't I listen? Why couldn't I just do it? So what if she turns me down? Maybe she isn't one bit interested, but I'll never know unless I try.

'Something the matter?' asks Dad.

'No,' I say. 'There's something I have to do.'

And do soon. The mocks are next week, so we're only in school part of the day, just for the exams.

'It's now or never.'

Dad looks confused.

'Now or never, what is?'

I think of Chloe. Suddenly I'm talking to myself.

'That's two things I have to do.'

'What are you on about?'

'Nothing. You just made me understand something about

myself. Listen Dad, I'm going after the thing I want most in the world. You've got to do it too. Tonight. You hear me? Right this minute.'

He's looking at me like I'm speaking fluent Bulgarian. But I don't care. I'm full of energy. I know what's got to be done. So things can be settled. So there can be The Happy Ending. So I can have closure.

'Now Dad. You're going to see Mum right now.'

Dad's still staring in a slightly bewildered way when I run out of the flat and on to the street.

Tuesday 5th December
7.00 p.m.

This is the hardest thing I've ever done. Chloe's looking right at me, eyes brimming with tears. Her pinched, pretty little face is red and blotchy.

'But why, Terry? What have I done wrong?'

'Nothing. You haven't done anything wrong.'

We're sitting on a wall at the top of her street. The blustery wind is whipping round us, showering us with icy raindrops. I zip my jacket up to the chin. I find myself biting on the zip, wishing I was somewhere else. What's going wrong? On the way up here, I had it all worked out. I've seen it in the movies. Boy meets girl. Boy loses girl. (To Fitz, rotten lousy mesomorphic stinkbag Fitz! OK, so that isn't in the movies, but what the heck, I had to get it off my chest.) Finally, boy wins girl. Life has a pattern. Love is written in the stars. Closing credits begin to roll with star billing to Manchester United. Happy ending.

'Then why do we have to split up?' asks Chloe in this whining, sniffly little voice that makes me want to scream. She grips my sleeve.

'Is there somebody else?'

Now she's dragging it out. I had this worked out too. She was meant to thank me for the good times and wish me well for the future. So why's she pulling my arm off and dribbling with misery?

'It's Julie Carter, isn't it?'

'No, she's got nothing to do with this . . .'

My voice trails off. I'm not sorry for her any more. I resent every reddened blotch on that pasty face of hers, every snotty sob from that pointy little nose. I'm impatient, angry. In fact, I want to run, to get away. I never wanted to hurt anybody. I made a mistake, a big one. I just want it put right, that's all. Why's she got to be like this?

The truth, it's the only way to set things right.

'OK, I really like Julie. It's always been her.'

Chloe lets out this miserable sob, but I carry on regardless. I'm talking to me now, not her.

'She probably doesn't know I exist, but . . .'

Chloe's got her face buried in her hands and her shoulders are shaking. I did that. Me! I never dreamed it could be this way. I thought that, if I ever split up with somebody, I'd be the one to end up heartbroken. Weird the way things turn out. Now I'm feeling sorry for her again.

'Chloe, don't. I'm not worth it, you see.'

I nearly burst out laughing. The stupidity of it. in the middle of this big scene I've just quoted a line from a song. Paul Young, I think. Some wrinkly from the eighties. Dad plays it when he's fed up. At my words, Chloe makes a noise like a wounded animal and her nose starts to run again. I pass her a handkerchief. She pushes my hand away.

'I don't want your rotten handkerchief!'

All of a sudden her voice sounds stronger. It crackles with resentment and wounded pride.

'I should never have trusted you, Terry Payne. You boys are all the same.'

I feel offended. Me, the same as Bobby? Me, the same as Fitz? Never!

'No, we're not. *I'm* not.'

'Yes, you are. You're like dogs.'

Dogs! So I'm a flipping labrador, am I?

'You can't stay loyal to one girl.'

But I can! I really can. I'm a good dog. But it's got to be the *right* girl. And that's what I say.

'I could stay loyal to Julie.'

Chloe's eyes fill with horror.

'I hate you, Terry.'

But that I can't take. I really am a good dog, the best dog. I could win Cruft's, I'm so good. I didn't want to hurt her. I don't want to be hated.

'Don't be like this, Chloe. We can still be friends.'

She gives an exasperated screech.

'No, Terry. No, we can't.'

She gets up to go.

'Hang on, Chloe, I've got something for you.'

I hold out the Man United Superstore carrier bag. Now I'm an expectant St Bernard. She stares at it as if I've just handed her a tin of Chum.

'I want you to have my presents. The receipt is still inside. You can get your money back. Buy something nice to cheer yourself up.'

Which is about as bad a line as any guy anywhere ever used to break up with a girl. Chloe stares in disbelief at the bag.

'You don't understand women, do you Terry?'

She slaps it away.

'Keep your stupid shirt.'

She walked away and stops outside her house.

'You know what, I hope you lose to Sturm Graz and I hope Liverpool batter you too!'

Which is the most she's ever said about football!

'Chloe . . .'

'I hope Michael Owen scores a hat-trick.'

Now that's in bad taste!

'Chloe . . .'

'And I hope Julie tells you to get stuffed.'

She goes inside and slams the front door behind her. Knowing my luck, Julie will probably do the same!

Wednesday 6th December
3.10 p.m.

Terry Payne, you have fifty minutes to save the universe.

Fifty minutes.

Three thousand seconds.

Three thousand six hundred heartbeats.

Listen to me, I'm starting to sound like Bobby. And the maths is probably wrong anyway! But the top and bottom of it is this: I have to pick Amy up from her school and rush her back to Knowsley Manor in time for footy practice. Tonight is the last practice of the year and I'm determined to stand up to Fitz, show him I'm not the weakest link. And somehow, in the middle of all that, I have to see Julie.

Tell her how I feel.

Before it's too late.

Wednesday 6th December
3.20 p.m.

This is too good to be true. I'm half-way up the hill, jogging past the police station, when I see Julie.

And she's crying.

Because of him?

It's got to be.

I run across the road with my sports bag in one hand and all my hopes and dreams in the other.

'Julie,' I stammer. 'Are you all right?'

It's the second time in two days I've been face to face with a girl in tears. I offer her a handkerchief, the *same* handkerchief. Unlike Chloe, she takes it.

'What's the matter?'

3.21 p.m. Nine minutes to pick up Amy. Thirty-nine minutes to save the universe.

'Nothing.'

'Come off it, you're crying.'

'It's nothing. I'm feeling a bit rough. I must be coming down with a cold.'

She does sound a bit under the weather, but that doesn't account for the tears.

'There's something else though, isn't there?'

'If you must know, it's Fitz.'

My heart feels like it's going to burst. Bobby was right.

'He can be such a pig. On my birthday too.'

'It's your birthday!'

Why didn't I know that? Why didn't somebody tell me?

158

3.22 p.m. Eight minutes to pick up Amy. Thirty-eight minutes to save the universe.

'What's he done?'

'He just comes on so strong. So pushy. Thinks he can order me around. He was so lovely at first. Now . . . Just because we're going out, it doesn't mean he owns me. Boys can be such . . .'

I remember what Chloe said.

'Dogs.'

Julie stares at me and laughs.

'What a funny thing to say!'

She says it so nicely I want to wag my tail. I remember the Huey, Louie and Duey crack. She thought that was funny too. Well, here goes nothing.

'Fitz doesn't deserve you.'

'No, and who does?'

There's a twinkle in her eye. She's teasing me. But in a nice way. There's a lump in my throat as big as a match ball. I can hardly swallow.

'Me. *I* deserve you.'

She stares at me for a second. Like I just landed from the Planet Loony Toon.

'You?'

'Yes, I really like you, Julie. I've always liked you.'

There, I've finally plucked up the courage. I've said it.

'What about Chloe?'

'It wasn't right. I finished with her. So I could ask you out.'

Now for the rejection, the big heave-ho. I close my eyes. But there's no rejection. I feel her hands on my shoulders! I feel her lips pressed against mine! It isn't a peck, either, this is a real, lingering, stay-in-the-mind smackeroo. Her fingers move down my chest, sending shivers of joy through me. I finally open my eyes.

'What was that for?'

'For being you. I just wish you'd said something earlier. *Four months earlier!* I didn't think you were interested. When you didn't make a move, I kind of let Kelly fix me up with Fitz. Everybody acted like it was going to happen anyway.'

Of course it was going to happen. Hasn't she seen all those

American high school movies? They'd be favourites for King and Queen of the Prom. But she's saying she'd have . . . I'm not imagining it, am I? She would have gone out with me! If I'd just asked. If only I'd asked. I stare at her, the moist, brown eyes, the full lips, the slightly reddened nose, the mane of raven hair.

'Me, not interested! I couldn't have been more interested. Didn't you see me looking at you? I couldn't take my eyes off you.'

Do I sound too needy? Oh, who cares? I *am* needy. I need you, Julie.

Julie smiles. A lovely smile. A heart-stopping smile. She liked me all the time! I think of all the wasted months, the pain of seeing her with Fitz. I'm such a loser.

'Are you and Fitz . . . ?'

'Finished? I don't know.'

I feel the air go cold between us. Julie seems to be having second thoughts. Let's face it, if she dumps him she loses the whole social circle around him.

No, don't have second thoughts. Stick with the first thoughts.

'Maybe I shouldn't be doing this.'

First thoughts!

First thoughts!

'No. You should! You should!'

She laughs. Her fingers are still on my chest. I can feel them right through my shirt, making my skin tingly and alive. I glance at my watch. 3.25 p.m. Five minutes to pick up Amy. Thirty-five minutes to save the universe.

Julie finally pulls away. I remember the scent of her hair, the press of her body. I can't let her go now.

'I don't know what I'm doing,' she says. 'This isn't fair on either of you.'

'But you're not meant to be with him. It isn't right.'

Julie smiles sadly.

'I don't know. Maybe you're right. Oh Terry, why didn't you say something earlier? Fitz can be a pain sometimes, but he really is a nice guy. He knows everybody. I don't want to hurt him, I don't want to hurt anyone.'

160

No, NO! You were doing fine when you said he was a pain. Hurt him. He's big and ugly enough.

'Terry, I'm confused.'

Confused! What's to be confused about? We're meant to be together. The kiss, Julie, remember the kiss.

I glance at my watch again. 3.26 p.m. Four minutes to pick up Amy. Thirty-four minutes to save the universe.

'Are you in a hurry?' she asks, a bit put out.

'No . . . Yes, I've got to pick up my little sister.'

Another own goal. Make a mental note: when you're opening your heart to the girl you love never, but never, look at your watch!

'You'd better go then. Here's my bus, anyway.'

I see the bus coming up the road. In my mind's eye, it's transformed into a steam train wreathed in clouds of white smoke. Julie and I are wearing matching trenchcoats and in the distance guns are booming. I know, I know, I've seen too many old movies, but somebody had to be there to hand Mum the Kleenex.

'Julie, don't go.'

'I've got to.'

She starts to run. I feel the burn of that kiss on my lips, every contour of her body against mine.

'You've got to finish with him, Julie. You've got to. We're meant to be together.'

There's a cluster of first-years at the stop. They giggle and point at me. They don't see the trenchcoats, so it must be the words that have set them off. Julie climbs on the bus. I watch it pull away. I search for her face in the windows.

In vain . . . She's gone . . . No, there she is, smiling, waving. There's a chance, a real chance for us. I glance at my watch. 3.29 p.m. A minute to pick up Amy. Thirty-one minutes to save the universe. But it's half-saved already. I told Julie how I felt and she didn't think about Man U. and Liverpool, and a love between two warring tribes. She didn't call me a loser or a weakest link. She didn't laugh.

She didn't do any of those things.

She kissed me.

Kissed . . . ME!

'I don't know why you bother,' sniffs Amy.

'It's because I'm going to get back in the team,' I tell her. 'Because . . .'

I think of Julie.

'Because I'm better than Fitz and I'm going to prove it.'

'It isn't even a proper match,' says Amy.

She's right. It's a practice match, but I don't care. Even if I were out on the pitch paying for United against Sturm Graz it couldn't be any more important. I've got to stand up to Fitz. I'll show him who the weakest link really is.

'OK lads,' shouts Six Guns, clapping his hands. 'Gather round.'

We're glad to. It's cold and wet and we just want to get started.

'Six-a-side. It's your mocks next week so we won't be getting together again until January. What I want to see tonight is commitment. We're playing Blackridge again on the 10th, so if you want to be in the side, show me what you're made of.'

When he comes to pick the sides, there's an A-team and a B-team. The A-team's got Fitz, Gary Tudor and Paul Scully. All we've got is Jamie Sneddon, Bobby and me. Hardly the sort of selection to make the earth move. As the game kicks off I see Kelly watching me. She's looking more like Sabrina than ever, but not as smiley. California Ice, that's Kelly Magee. She's glaring at me. I wonder if she senses that something's happened between Julie and me. She's always known that Julie felt something too. Of course, that's why she gave me such a hard time because she knew it was a two-way thing!

But there's no time to worry about that now. Gary Tudor's coming towards me.

'Go to him, Bobby,' I shout. 'I'll take Fitz.'

Gary lays it off before Bobby can close him down. It's a straight contest between me and Fitz. Just when it looks like he's getting away from me, I wrap my leg round the ball and force it out for a throw-in. Fitz looks put out. From the throw-

162

in, he tries to go past me again, but I'm ready for him. He tries the nutmeg.

'You are the weakest link,' he says.

But I get the block on. There's no goodbye. He has a dig at me as he walks away.

'I saw that,' says Bobby.

'Forget it, Bob,' I tell him. 'Just shows he's not getting his own way.'

Two minutes later Fitz is through again. I'm the last man. He chips the ball over my head and goes after it. I don't have his pace, but I'm not letting him get away. I lean into him and throw him off balance.

'Foul!' he roars, but Six Guns isn't having any.

'Play on.'

The moment Six Guns turns away, Fitz elbows me in the ribs.

'You've had it,' he warns.

I shove him away.

'Rattled?' I ask.

I remember Julie's lips pressed against mine. Who's the weakest link now, Fitz?

It's some time before we find ourselves in the same area of the pitch again, but this time we're both fired up. We go for a fifty-fifty ball. Nobody is going to pull out of this challenge. I see his studs go up. The idiot, he could do me some serious damage.

'You are the weakest link,' he hisses.

But I'm not backing down. I raise my feet just as high as he has. We're on collision course.

'Goodbye!'

The crunch is sickening. My shin hurts a bit as I hop away from the collision, but I've come through pretty much un-scathed. I see the ball bobble away. There's a strange noise coming from underneath me, but I can't quite focus on it. I'm too excited. I did it. I put one over on Fitz. But just as I'm picking myself up I hear the scream. It's him. He's underneath me, lying awkwardly.

And he's screaming.

He's not faking it, either.

163

He's in agony.

'Look what you've done!' roars Gary Tudor, facing up to me. 'You did that on purpose. You maniac!'

I look around. Everybody is staring at me eyes cold with anger and accusation.

'It was fifty-fifty,' I protest. 'He raised his studs first.'

They're all shouting, all of them except Bobby.

'Knock it off, will you?' yells Six Guns. 'You're not doing anybody any good. Run for the school secretary, somebody. This looks bad. I think he's broken his ankle.'

Broken it? Oh no, not that!

I look down at Fitz. What have I done?

I see Kelly on her mobile. I know who she's phoning. It's Julie. It's got to be. I can just see her nursing her cold and hearing this. What's she going to think? On no! Not this, not now. Not when everything was going my way. I can feel the other lads jostling me, letting me know what they think of the tackle. But I don't care. It's not just Fitz who's lying broken on the ground. It's all my hopes. Julie will never believe it was an accident. She'll never believe me.

I *am* the weakest link.

Goodbye.

Thursday 7th December
9.00 a.m.

'What do you mean, you're not going? My band is playing again.'

'I mean, I'm not going. Not after last night.'

The last place I want to be tomorrow is the Christmas disco. I'd be the rotten turkey. Not only did I put Fitz in hospital and wreck things with Julie, but Mum told Dad she wasn't interested in getting back together. You know what she told him: *You've hurt me too much*. United beat Sturm Graz 2–0 last night and I hardly even noticed!

'People will soon forget.'

I indicated Paul Scully and Jamie Sneddon. They're shaking their heads. I know it's for my benefit.'

'Do they look as if they're going to forget?'

I see Kelly and Gary Tudor coming the other way. No sign of Julie.

'How's Fitz?' I ask.

'What do you care?' snaps Gary. 'That tackle was out of order.'

'I didn't do it on purpose,' I protest.

'That's not what Fitz thinks,' says Kelly. Then, with venom: 'Or Julie.'

'Where is she anyway?'

'She's got a heavy cold. She's staying off till Monday. She wants to be better for the mocks.'

'What did she say?'

'About you? Nothing. Who do you think you are?'

'I don't believe you, Payne,' says Gary. 'Doing something like that to a team-mate, just because you're jealous.'

'I'm not jealous!'

'Not much you're not,' says Kelly. 'Julie's told me about you following her around.'

Julie told Kelly! She wouldn't. Not after what she said to me last night.

'You're off your head,' says Gary, walking away.

'Kelly,' I say, as she starts to follow.

'What?'

'What did Julie really say?'

Kelly shakes her head.

'Gary's right. You are off your head.'

And that's it. I'm standing with a face like a smacked behind. Chloe walks past and adds her own two-pennyworth.

'Happy now?' she asks. 'Dumper gets dumped, eh?'

Right now, I want to be anywhere but here in the school corridor.

'What was that?' asks Bobby.

'What?'

'Pleading with Kelly like that. Haven't you got any pride?'

Maybe not. So I stand among the jostling kids feeling like I've had my guts kicked out. Just yesterday afternoon everything seemed to be going my way. How could it all go so wrong so quickly?

Thursday 7th December
9.30 p.m.

'Mum,' I ask. 'Are you serious?'

'Serious about what?'

'Dad, of course.'

Mum looks up from her book.

'Yes, Terry, I'm serious. I don't see any way back for us.'

'But he's . . .'

'What?'

'He's sorry.'

'Sorry! That's a good one. Terry, you say sorry for dropping a plate. Sorry is nowhere near good enough after what he's done to me. I built my life around that man. Don't you understand? I put everything into this family. I lost track of most of my friends. I didn't need them, did I? I had Geoff. Well, I look pretty stupid now, don't I?'

'Don't be like this,' I say.

'So how do you want me to be?' Mum demands. 'I dare say you'd like me to welcome him back with open arms.'

She lays on the sarcasm with a trowel.

'Hello honey, welcome home. Sorry I don't give you the butterflies any more. I'll try to get my act together. How many pounds would you like me to lose? Thirty? I'll do my best. Sit down, my lord and master, while I get you a cup of tea.'

'But he's dumped Mule.'

'Well hallelujah!' cries Mum. 'Now he's dumped two women. Doesn't that make me feel better!'

I throw back my head. She sees the look on my face and places a hand on my shoulder.

'I'm sorry, Terry, I shouldn't pile all this on you, but you have to understand, Geoff's hurt me. It isn't something you can put right just like that.'

Amy comes downstairs.

'Are you two arguing?'

'Arguing?' says Mum, 'No love. Just talking.'

'Funny,' says Amy. 'You talk to Terry like you used to talk to Dad.'

We watch her going back upstairs.

166

'Not daft, is she?' I say.

'No,' says Mum. 'She's growing up fast.'

Friday 8th December
7.00 p.m.

I'm standing in the drenching rain where I kissed Julie three days and a whole lifetime ago, reliving the joy, the hope. Across the road, I can see kids making their way towards school to the Christmas disco. Gary and Kelly are jogging, sharing an umbrella. Paul Scully and Pepsey Cooper are just behind them. Everybody has somebody, everyone but me. Then I get another shock.

I see Jamie Sneddon coming up the road straight towards me. I know the girl who's with him too.

'Chloe?'

'Well, if it isn't Terry,' she says acidly. 'Julie not coming tonight? Oh no, I forgot. She'll be feeding Fitz a bunch of grapes and signing his plaster cast.'

Jamie hangs around waiting for her. He looks uncomfortable. When you catch a girl on the rebound, you don't want to be too close to her ex.

'How does it feel to be a loser, Terry?'

She comes closer.

'Maybe now you understand how you made me feel.'

With that she links arms with Jamie and clatters away on her high heels.

'Great,' I say out loud. 'Just great.'

What happened to the pattern, the Happy Ending?

At that very moment I see Bobby crossing the road towards me.

'Was that Chloe?'

'Yes, Jamie's taking her.'

'She doesn't let the grass grow.'

I nod.

'Caitlin told me you were here,' says Bobby. 'What do you think you're doing?'

I shrug.

'I'm not quite sure myself.'

167

'Come to the disco.'

'Joking, aren't you? There's no Alison for me tonight.'

Bobby chuckles.

'You needn't worry. We're not playing it tonight. Come on, you'll enjoy yourself.'

'I doubt it. Chloe's just had a pop at me.'

'Big deal. Girls come and girls go. You're taking it all too seriously. Come on Terry. Check out the talent. Emma Holland's all right you know, and she's unattached.'

'I don't think so, Bobby.'

I turn to go.

'Snap out of it, Terry. These things happen.'

As if to add to my misery, a car passes playing Travis' 'Why does it always rain on me?'

'Don't listen to it,' says Bobby. 'Who needs victim-rock?'

'Victims,' I say pointedly.

With that, I set off home, leaving the spot where I very nearly made Julie mine.

Saturday 9th December
2.50 p.m.

Dad lets me in.

In the background I can hear: 'Don't dream it's over' by Crowded House. He's getting into the victim-rock as well.

'That bad, huh?' I ask.

'She just blew me out, Terry, told me she wasn't interested.'

'You walked out on her, remember.'

'But I thought . . .'

'She'd be falling over herself to take you back? You're forgetting the little matter of a woman called Mule. Mum's got some pride, you know. Nobody wants to be second-best to somebody who uses Permatan.'

'But you told me to go and see her.'

'And I was right to. You can still get her back.'

'I don't know,' he says, shaking his head. 'So how's Chloe?'

'I broke it off.'

'Yes?'

168

'Yes. I finished it and told Julie how I felt.'

'Julie?'

'The girl I really care about. I must have told you.'

Dad frowns.

'Can't recall. So you're going out with this Julie now?'

'No. I crippled her boyfriend.'

'What?!'

I manage to explain, after a fashion, just before kick-off.

'I don't think either one of us is much of a Romeo,' says Dad. 'Let's see if we can do better at football.'

United are at Charlton. I'm at a low ebb after the Julie debacle. I need a good performance. At least the Red Devils can come up with a Happy Ending. Just minutes into the match, it doesn't look like I'll get it. Charlton score the opening goal and it could be three. Our defence is all over the place.

'Nothing's going right,' says Dad, hurling a shoe across the room. I notice that he's got a hole in his sock.

Who's arguing? He's right, nothing is going right. I can't get Chloe's words out of my head. In my mind's eye, I see Julie feeding Fitz grapes and adjusting his pillow. We're 1–0 down, our nearest challengers Arsenal are 2–0 up, Mum's sent Dad away with a flea in his ear and I've blown it with Julie. Not the best two days of my life.

'Come on, United!'

We steady the ship and launch wave after wave after attacks, but with half-time approaching we're still behind.

'Come on, lads. Fight for it!'

Which is just what they do. Suddenly we score twice in thirty-five seconds, Giggs and Solskjaer. In the second half Roy Keane hits a screamer.

'3–1! Ye-e-e-ss!'

Fight for it! That's what I've got to do with Julie. Forget the way I behaved last night, I refuse to lie down.

'We'll stay eight points ahead of Arsenal,' I say, but I've spoken too soon. Fergie has taken Keane and Beckham off, saving them for the Liverpool game next week. Is it too soon? Looks like it. Charlton pull one back. 3–2 and a jittery last ten minutes.

'It's not over,' says Dad.

Oh no, even when you fight for it things go wrong. And they do go wrong. Big style. Charlton equalise.

'I don't believe it,' groans Dad.

Neither do I. No matter what I do, everything just falls apart. The pair of us sit there, staring disaster and possible defeat in the face.

'Fight for it, lads,' I shout, as much for me and Dad as for United.

We're into injury time. Three minutes added on. Backs to the wall.

Fight for it.

Giggs fizzes a shot wide.

Sixty seconds left.

Fight for it. For goodness sake, fight for it.

There's no time left. We draw 3–3 and lose ground at the top.

'I feel sick,' says Dad.

'Me too,' I admit. 'Now we've got to beat Liverpool next Sunday, or Arsenal could be just three points behind us.'

I think of the old enemy, then of Julie and Fitz.

I *will* fight for it.

8

The build-up starts here.

I take a deep breath and walk into school. The hall and the dreaded Maths paper are waiting for me at the end of this corridor. Julie too, if she's feeling better. What do I say to her? How do I make her understand? If I could get her on her own, maybe, just maybe, I could get her to listen. Fat chance of that, though. Kelly's bound to be there protecting her form the Mad Manc (my new nickname). I haven't even got Bobby for company. He's late.

'Here goes nothing,' I murmur to nobody in particular.

In the event, it's even worse than I'd been expecting. Julie hasn't just got Kelly round her, but Fitz is there too. Look at him, milking the attention for all he's worth. He's standing propped up on his crutches, holding court to Gary and Paul. Before you can say wounded hero, Pepsey rolls up to sign his cast. Then, just to pile on the agony, Jamie and even Chloe join the admiring crowd.

'Look what the cat's just dragged in,' scoffs Gary.

'Maimed anyone today?' sneers Paul.

He pretends to fall over.

'See that, he just chopped me.'

Everybody's laughing, even Chloe. Especially Chloe. No, scrub that, Julie isn't laughing, but who knows whether that's a good thing or a bad one. Her face is completely expressionless.

'Now now,' says Fitz, surprising everybody by his response. 'Go easy, eh? It was a fifty-fifty ball. I was unlucky, that's all.'

Gary's mouth is hanging open.

171

'No hard feelings, Terry.'

With that, Fitz makes his way to his table. The heads of his entourage turn to follow their hero. He's stunned them to silence. Me too. As I sit down and stare at the test paper lying face down in front of me, I hear the hall door open. It's Bobby, closely followed by Caitlin. I frown questioningly.

'Don't ask,' Bobby hisses. 'Just don't ask.'

He and Caitlin sit at opposite ends of the hall, about as far apart as they could get.

'Settle down, please,' says Six Guns.

He's no need to say that, the place is like a mausoleum already. He runs through the usual preamble, then gives the fatal order:

'Begin.'

I flick through the paper.

Finding the nth term.

Gulp.

Three-letter Angle Notation.

Eek.

Combinations of Transformations.

Come again.

Vectors.

Mayday, mayday, the SS Terry is sinking fast.

Loci and Constructions.

Latest news. SS Terry is lost with all hands. Next of kin have been informed.

I look around. Fitz is beavering away already. Julie is writing too. Caitlin meets my eye then looks away with a toss of her reddish hair. I realise with horror that everybody knows what they're doing except me.

SS Terry hits the ocean bottom.

Completely sunk.

Monday 11th December
11.15 a.m.

'How do you think it went?' asks Bobby.

'What?'

'The exam, you dufus.'

172

'I didn't,' I say. 'It was rock hard.'

'Funny, I don't think it was that bad,' he says.

'It wasn't,' I tell him, 'so long as you've got a brain. Which I haven't.'

I mime opening my skull.

'See, cranial cavity completely empty. Anyway, what's with you and Caitlin?'

'We're finished,' says Bobby. 'Cheeky little cow. She only nicked my mobile and found Rosie's number.'

'You mean . . . ?'

'That's right, now they've both dumped me.'

'I did warn you,' I say, but Bobby's miles away.

'Bobby, are you listening?'

'Back in a minute,' he says.

'But where . . . ?'

Now I know where. He's gone over to talk to Emma Holland, the one he tried to pair me off with on Friday. I don't believe that lad! He doesn't stay dumped for long. Now what's he doing? He writing something down. She's given him her phone number!

He looks round and grins before walking out towards the bus stop with Emma. I'm still marvelling at his ability to bounce back from a dumping when Fitz arrives. We're alone in the corridor.

'Thanks for what you said . . .' I begin, before he cuts me off.

'That was for my public,' he says. 'Now for the authorised version. You're a mad get, you know that? I had a trial this week with Liverpool and you've put me out for weeks. I hope you're proud of yourself.'

'But you said . . .'

'I know what I said, and Julie will love me for it. She's into all that forgiveness stuff. Not me. Believe me, you're going to pay for what you did, Payne.'

He checks the corridor then shoves his face into mine.

'I know you've been hanging round my girl. Well, forget it. You're pond-life, Payne, and I'm going to make sure Julie knows it. Before I've finished, she'll think you're responsible for the Ebola virus, the thinning of the ozone layer and global warming! My Dad's treating us this Sunday.'

He pulls a couple of tickets

'Man U. v. Liverpool. That's right, I'm taking Julie, and we're going to watch the boys stuff your lot. You're a loser, Payne, always were, always will be.'

There's more to come, but just as Fitz is warming to his theme Julie and Kelly start walking towards us. Fitz takes a step backwards and his voice changes completely.

'So like I say, no hard feelings. It could have been you in a plaster cast.'

He shoots out a hand and pumps mine.

'See you, Terry. Oh, and good luck this Sunday.'

He winks.

'You'll need it.'

Julie walks past me without saying a word. It's only when I hear the main door slam that I realise I should have said something, anything, to put my side of the story.

Now it's too late.

Thursday 14th December
12.30 p.m.

So much for the pattern of life. I had it all worked out: Boy meets girl. Girl meets ratbag. Girl ditches ratbag for boy. Boy and girl live happily ever after. Well, if there's one thing I've learned about the pattern it's this:

THERE IS NO PATTERN.

Stuff happens. Not just good stuff, either. Bad stuff, stupid stuff, stuff to make you squirm, stuff to make your toes curl, how-on-earth-could-that-happen stuff.

Just stuff.

'Penny for them,' says Bobby before stuffing half a burger in his mouth.

'I was just thinking,' I tell him. 'All this Happy Ever After rubbish. It's a complete con. What you get in real life is just any old Ever After. Happy doesn't come into it.'

We set off towards school. It's French this afternoon. Sacre flipping bleu!

'Is this about Julie?' Bobby asks, 'Or Liverpool beating Fulham last night?'

I grimace. I sat through Liverpool's victory sinking deeper and deeper into despair.

'Both.'

It's all the same thing. Not only did Liverpool win, but Julie's hero Michael Owen bounced back from injury to score the opening goal. When he scored, it was like watching Fitz celebrate. Just what I needed only five days before the United–Liverpool match. I remember what Chloe said: *I hope he scores a hat-trick*.

'You know your problem?' says Bobby. 'You take things too seriously. Just have a laugh, like me.'

I see this cartoon picture of Bobby being booted out of one door by Caitlin and Rosie only to bounce right back into another door opened by a smiling Emma Holland.

'I'd definitely be happier,' I admit. 'But I wouldn't be me, would it?'

'I suppose you're right,' says Bobby. 'You're the loyal, decent sort. All sincerity and moral dilemmas.'

Then, with a mischievous grin, he adds: 'Poor sod!'

We reach the school gates. There's Fitz sitting on a bench. Julie and Kelly are sitting either side of him. Gary, Pepsey and Paul are standing.

'Poor performance,' Gary's saying. 'I mean, Fulham might be top of the Nationwide, but they out-passed us for half the match.'

Fitz sees me coming.

'Maybe,' he says, 'But at least we showed a bit of steel. Patient for ninety minutes, then bam, bam, bam, three in extra time. We didn't throw late goals away.'

Unlike United at Charlton.

'And Owen's back. Lethal weapon.'

'So you think we'll turn United over on Sunday?' asks Kelly, also aware of my presence.

'Flatten 'em,' says Fitz. 'Oh, hello Terry, didn't see you there. Did I mention that Julie and I were going to Old Trafford? Have you got a ticket?'

'You know I haven't.'

'Well, just stay in front of the TV. You might even see us on the screen. We'll give you a wave.'

I glance at Julie but she doesn't return the look. I've been tried and convicted before a no-jury kangaroo court.

Charge: that you, Terry Payne, on or about 16.40 hours on Wednesday, 6th December, did, with malice aforethought, break the ankle of one John Fitzpatrick.

Verdict: that the above-mentioned rotten, lousy Manc is guilty of actual bodily harm, driven by acute jealousy and general low character.

Sentence: that you, Terry Payne, be left unloved and unwanted for the rest of your natural life. On the lesser charge of being a rotten, lousy Manc you are further sentenced to watch your team getting thumped by a resurgent Liverpool FC.

What I need now to put Fitz in his place is a magnificent reposte, a gem of wit and repartee.

'Fitz,' I say, after a moment's thought, 'Get stuffed.'

Friday 15th December
3.30 p.m.

'Oh, give it a rest, will you?' says Bobby. 'All you talk about is Julie, Julie, Julie. Get over it, will you?'

'I don't want to get over it,' I shoot back. 'She likes me, I mean really likes me. We could be good together, special. It'd be criminal if she stayed with a slimeball like Fitz just because of a misunderstanding.'

'I think,' Bobby says, correcting me, 'that it's because of the broken ankle.'

'I wish I was the one with the broken ankle,' I say wistfully. 'Then everything would be all right.'

'You have got it bad, haven't you?' says Bobby. 'OK, if you won't move on, why not talk to her?'

'How?' I cry. 'I can't get her on her own. If it isn't Fitz hanging round her, it's Kelly. There's always somebody on guard.'

'Phone her,' says Bobby.

'I don't know her number. And she's ex-directory. I checked.'

Bobby scrolls down the addresses on his mobile.

'There you go,' he says, flashing the screen at me.

'What are you doing with her number?' I ask suspiciously.

'I got it when she started at our school,' says Bobby. 'She's a looker. I was interested too.'

I give him daggers.

'Hey, you should be thanking me. The moment you told me how you felt, I backed off.'

'You *were* going out with Caitlin at the time,' I remind him.

'OK, that too. Look, do you want this number or not?'

I write it down. I read the magic numbers. Time to take the plunge.

Friday 15th December
4.00 p.m.

My mobile isn't charged so I have to wait for Mum to get off the phone.

'Oh, come on,' I say.

'She's talking to Dad,' says Amy.

'Really?'

'They've been talking for ages.'

'What about?'

'He's asking to come home.'

'How do you know?'

'I was listening on the upstairs extension until they chased me.'

I smile. I always thought Amy was getting along just fine with our semi-detached family. Seems she's as keen as me for them to get back together.

'Think there's much chance?' Amy asks.

The words are no sooner out of her mouth when Mum slams down the receiver.

'That answer your question?' I say.

Amy retires to her room. I wait until Mum's gone before punching in Julie's number.

'Hello?'

It's a boy voice. Either Huey, Duey or Louie. I mean, Gerard, Josh or John-Joe.

'Is Julie there?'

'Who's asking?'

'It's Terry.'

'Oh, you're the Mad Manc, aren't you? Fitzy's told us all about you.'

'So can I speak to her?'

'No. And, by the way, we're going to flatten you on Sunday.'

The line goes dead.

Friday 15th December
4.45 p.m.

With any luck, Julie's three-headed guard dog will have gone out by now.

'Hello?'

It's the second head, another boy's voice, deeper than last time.

'Could I speak to Julie please?'

'Who's asking?'

'Terry.'

'Oh, the . . .'

'Yes, the Mad Manc. Now could I speak to her?'

'No chance. You're going to get battered this Sunday.'

Friday 15th December
5.15 p.m.

I've got to have more luck this time.

'Hello.'

Damn! The third head. The youngest by the sound of it.

'Could I speak to Julie, please?'

'No, you can't, you Mad Manc . . .'

'I know,' I say, cutting him short, 'We're going to get hammered this Sunday.'

This time I hang up myself.

Friday 15 December
6.00 p.m.

I run to answer the phone. Maybe Julie's seen the light. It's got to be. Yes, that's it, she's slipped to the phone box to escape the attentions of her brothers. (I can dream, can't I?)

But it's only Bobby.

'Oh, hi.'

'So,' he asks. 'How did it go?'

'It didn't. I keep getting her brothers on the line.'

'Why don't you ring her mobile?'

'You've got her mobile number!'

'Sure have.'

He must have fancied her more than he's been letting on. I don't say anything. I just want the number. He reels it off.

'Why didn't you give it to me in the first place?'

Bobby sounds apologetic.

'I didn't think. Anyway, I've got to go. I'm taking Emma out.'

I hang up and phone Julie's mobile. My heart misses a beat. It's ringing and there are no brothers to field the call. But there is Fitz. I'd know his voice anywhere.

'Hello?'

I can't think what to say.

'Hello?'

I hear him talking to Julie.

'I just answered your mobile, Ju, but they're not speaking.'

There's a moment's pause then a note of suspicion enters his voice.

'That isn't the Mad Manc, is it?'

I can hear Julie in the background. So near and yet so far. I hang up without answering.

Saturday 16th December
3.50 p.m.

I've felt lower, but I can't remember when. I'm round at my Dad's, and that's about as much fun as putting my leg through a bacon slicer lately. He took me and Amy for a pizza earlier.

We had plans to take a walk round Sherdley Park or something but it's throwing it down as usual, so Amy wanted to go home. I look out of the window at the downpour. Why *does* it always rain on me? I read the footy pages again. Every time I look at the Liverpool line-up for tomorrow they look stronger. I mean, those three strikers, Heskey, Fowler and, of course, Owen. And we still look shaky at the back. Those three goals we shipped against Charlton. Then there's the shortage of strikers on our side. Cole injured, Yorke suspended. Oh, stop torturing your-self, Terry lad. It's the mighty Reds at Old Trafford. Unbeaten since dinosaurs walked the Earth. It's ten years since Liverpool turned us over there. March 1990. But the record's got to go some time. Why not tomorrow?

'Got myself in a right mess, haven't I?' says Dad, breaking the silence.

'Come again.'

'Walking out on your mother. What was I thinking of?'

'Maybe it's going to take time,' I say, feeling more than a bit impatient.

If I've had to put up with his whingeing once, I've had to listen to it a thousand times. I ought to say something but I can't pluck up the courage.

'Nobody likes to feel second best,' I tell him.

I feel a pang of guilt as I remember the night I dumped Chloe.

'Is that what she said?'

'She didn't have to, Dad. Mule was everything Mum wanted to be. She could get in a size 12 for a start, and she had you.'

Dad buries his head in his hands and puts on his suicide tape. He's done this compilation of misery-rock: the Verve, Crowded House, R. Kelly, REM. That's it, if he's going to wallow in self-pity, I'm off. With United playing tomorrow, I can't even distract him by putting the footy on the radio. As I hit the street I zip my jacket up to my chin and pull my cap low over my eyes. It's sheeting down and it's cold. I squint through the silvery, flickering rain and look ahead to the holiday.

Julie and Fitz at Old Trafford.

Julie and Fitz exchanging presents on Christmas Day.

Julie and Fitz exchanging kisses at the stroke of twelve on New Year's Eve.

I see her lovely face at all the high points of the calendar and I know she'll be doing them all without me. For a moment I feel like going back to listen to the suicide tape with Dad. But I've sworn that I'm not going to give in. Somehow, some way I'm going to fight for her. She's too good for Fitz. She doesn't even really want to be with him. That stupid challenge! It pushed her back into his arms. One moment of madness, and my life's gone pear-shaped.

'I'm depending on you, lads,' I say out loud.

I can't bear the thought of Fitz triumphant. If Liverpool wins tomorrow he'll have it all. A victory over my team, my place in the school side, my girl by his side.

'You can't let me down,' I say.

I'm walking down Oliver Lyme Road. This old dear gives me a suspicious look. People get really paranoid about lads who talk to themselves. I let her get further up the road before clenching my fists and announcing to the world:

'You've got my happiness in your hands, boys. You've got to beat them, tank them, flatten them, murder them!'

Got to.

Sunday 17th December
11.14 a.m.

I have a bad feeling about this. They've just announced that Teddy Sheringham is out with a hamstring problem. That leaves us with only one fit striker, Ole Solskjaer. Liverpool will never have a better chance of turning us over.

'Another injury,' groans Dad. 'Doesn't anything ever go right?'

I'm dying to tell him to stop moaning, but I feel kind of sorry for him, so I bite my tongue. Besides, I'm too busy scanning the Old Trafford crowd for some sign of Julie and Fitz. The TV presenters keep repeating Gerard Houllier's words: 'We're going to beat them one day.' One day, but not today. Please not today.

'If we lose,' says Dad handing me a bowl of crisps and

181

cashew nuts, 'my life won't be worth living. It's all Liverpool lads at work.'

'I know,' I say through gritted teeth. 'You keep telling me.'

Doesn't he ever stop moaning?

The match kicks off. For the first half hour it's like a game of chess. Liverpool are defending deep and stopping us playing. We can't get our natural rhythm going.

'Great,' says Dad. 'Even United are letting me down now.'

Letting you down. Since when was it about you, Dad? Stop rotten moaning!

He's right about one thing, though. We're not playing well. The only decent chances go to Liverpool. We're not opening them up at all. With forty minutes gone, Fitz and Julie will be well pleased. Liverpool are holding their own at Old Trafford.

'Too many passes going astray,' says Dad. 'If we lose . . .'

Stop moaning!

A couple of minutes before half-time things take a big turn for the worse. Gary Neville handles the ball outside the penalty area. It's a free kick in a dangerous position. Danny Murphy hits a curving shot just inside the post. We're 1–0 down. I flop back in my chair. I can just see Fitz with his arms round Julie. I'm just wishing that voodoo dolls worked when my mobile goes.

'What's the score, Terry?'

It's him, Fitz. He's called me from Old Trafford just to wind me up.

'Make sure you stay tuned at half-time,' he chuckles. 'You do want to see the goal again, don't you?'

I hang up on him. How did he get my number anyway? Stupid question, I suppose. After all, I got Julie's.

'Who was that?'

'Nobody.'

A big, grinning nobody.

There's no respite after the interval. After just one minute Michael Owen hits the bar.

'This is going from bad to worse,' says Dad.

Honestly, I've never really noticed until the last few weeks, but he could whine for England!

Stop moaning, stop moaning, stop moaning!

A minute later Solskjaer almost scores at the other end, our first meaningful attempt on goal.

'It's not our day,' whines Dad. 'We're not going to do it.'

Quit it, quit it, quit it!

Westerveld comes off his line to thwart Scholes.

'We can't lose, not to them.'

For goodness' sake, Dad, shut up.

We press and we press, but there's no penetration. After a frustrating second half we're seconds away from our first home defeat to Liverpool for ten years. Sure enough, the whistle goes and that's it, we've lost. If Arsenal beat Spurs tomorrow night we'll only be three points clear at the top of the table. That's when I see them. It's Fitz and Julie all right, wearing matching Liverpool away strips. The Sky Sports cameramen do this, zooming in on a cute girl. Only the cute girl they've chosen today is having the face kissed off her by my mortal enemy. He looks straight at the camera and holds up his fingers to signal 1–0. I know it's meant for me. It's what he promised. I stare at Julie. I wouldn't say she looks unhappy. How could she be? Her team has just won a famous victory. But there's a tension. I'm not kidding myself, am I? Even here, amid scenes of jubilation, she's not quite sure if it's him she wants to be with. Am I reading too much into a slight change of expression? I'm starting to know you, Julie Carter, and you don't really believe he's the one, do you? In the midst of despair I give a half-smile.

'What are you grinning at?' demands Dad. 'Don't you realise what's just happened? This is the worst day of my life.'

And, at long last, I say it:

'If this is the worst day of your life, you've had it pretty easy,' I snap. 'Just stop whining, Dad.'

He stares in disbelief.

'Whining? I've lost the woman I love, I'm living in a dump and now my team's lost to Liverpool.'

'It's true. You've lost Mum, but whose fault is that, Dad? Nobody asked you to walk out. Stop looking for excuses. You did it, nobody else. So stop whining and do something about it.'

I'm half-way to the door when he grabs my sleeve.

'You've no right to talk to me like that,' he says.

'Haven't I?'

I'm feeling strong. Even here, even after the bitterest setback of the season, I know it's not over. We're still top of the Premiership and Julie's still the same girl who said she had feelings for me.

'We're all responsible for our own actions, Dad. You made a mistake, so put it right. Things happen because we let them. Well, I'm not going to lie down and die. I'm going to fight for what I want. Maybe you should do the same.'

Dad stands open-mouthed. I've said what I wanted, so I turn on my heel and jog down the stairs to the street. As I walk past the library and the museum I can feel the hurt of the defeat and of Fitz hugging Julie like that. But I won't let it end this way. Julie and me, we're meant to be together. I know it and somewhere, deep down, I think she does too. You want the Happy Ending, Terry Payne? Well, it won't just drop into your lap. Like you said to the old man, you're going to have to fight for it.

Eveything's still to play for.

Terry and Julie's story continues in the
second part of this story:
Julie and Me . . . Treble Trouble.
Read on for an extract from this exciting new book.

Julie and Me . . . Treble Trouble

Alan Gibbons

1

There are two loves in my life: Julie Carter and Manchester United FC. The Reds are no problem. They've returned every ounce of love I've given them, and more. With every flowing, pulsating attack, with every telling pass and every goal, they tell me I matter. I'm part of the Red Tribe, a winner. It's different with Julie. With every flick of her glossy, black mane of hair, every sulky glance from those deep, brown eyes, she cuts me to the quick, tells me I'm nothing. She's going out with somebody else – total pond-life – and it's just breaking my heart.

'Any score, Terry?' shouts Mum.

She isn't really bothered about football, it's more a matter of moral support. She knows what I'll be like if we lose.

'Still 0–0.'

I'm pacing the kitchen floor, listening to United–Ipswich on the radio. After three thousand, two hundred and forty minutes of football, two hundred and ninety-six fouls, twenty-eight bookings and one hundred and thirty-three goals, we finally lost our two-year unbeaten home record to Liverpool last week. It's vital we bounce back with a win today.

'Amy and I are nipping down to the shops,' says Mum, sticking her head round the door. 'I don't think we've got enough milk for the holiday.'

'OK.'

That's all there is of the Payne household at the moment, me, Amy and Mum. My dad walked out last summer, saying he 'didn't get the butterflies any more.' He seems to have got them back all of a sudden just lately, though. He goes soppy every time I mention Mum's name. He makes out he's fallen in love with her all over again and he wants to come home, but – and here's the thunderbolt – Mum doesn't want to know. He's made his bed, she reckons, so he can lie in it.

The change of heart came as quite a surprise. For months it's been Mum who's been the needy one, wanting him back, wishing he'd reconsider. But in the last few weeks she's had a change of heart. I've noticed something different about her, as if she's looked at herself in the mirror and decided to take hold of her life. Good for her, scary for Dad.

The doorbell goes. It's my best mate, Bobby Quinn.

'Room for a little one?' he asks, with the usual twinkle in his eye.

'I thought you'd be out with Emma,' I grunt.

Emma Holland is his latest girlfriend.

'She's in Liverpool, shopping with her mum and sister. What's the score at Old Trafford?'

'0–0.'

'Everton?'

That's Bobby's team. He's a bit of a masochist, my mate.

'Losing 1–0.'

He doesn't look surprised. Well, who would?

'Liverpool did you a favour this morning, didn't they Terry?'

Not half. After beating us last week at Old Trafford, and very nearly cutting my soul to ribbons, they've just hammered our closest rivals Arsenal 4–0 at Anfield. Weird thing, football. Your worst enemies can become allies overnight. Nothing is ever black and white. A bit like life, really.

'Doing anything over Christmas?' asks Bobby.

'No, family stuff, that's all. You?'

'A couple of parties. I'm taking Emma. That's what I called round for, to see if you wanted to come. The first one's tonight.'

'What, and play gooseberry? No thanks.'

'You can't just sit at home moping over Julie. You know your trouble? You've put her on a pedestal.'

Put here there? She climbed up all by herself.

'She's a girl, Terry, not an angel, not a vision, a flesh and blood girl. There's plenty more just like her.'

Like Julie? No, Bobby, not for me.

'Get back out in the field. I did.'

Didn't he just! For weeks he was dating two girls at once. No sooner had they rumbled him and given him the elbow than he was copping off with Emma. Mr Rebound, that's Bobby, an elastic-band Romeo. He doesn't understand me at all. It's all a game to him. He doesn't see how you can set your heart on just one girl. He's never fallen for anyone the way I've fallen for Julie. Love at first sight means different things to different people. For me it meant wanting Julie until it hurt. For Bobby it meant loving himself.

'Forget it, Bobby,' I tell him. 'Not interested.'

The roar of the crowd alerts me to a goal-scoring opportunity. 1–0. Ole . . . Gunner . . . Solskjaer. I dance round the kitchen, arms raised. The Reds . . . returning the love. I wish Julie was. But she's with Fitz, John Fitzpatrick, the most popular kid in Year 11, captain of the football team and all-round hunk. I think of him, a kind of cross between Brad Pitt and Michael Owen, and then me, a mini Chris Evans, and I know I've got no chance with Julie. She's out of my league. Solskjaer's through again. 2–0. He is my Solskjaer, my Ole Solskjaer.

'We're back,' I crow. 'We're back.'

I'm back too. Last week, I was dead and buried. I'd lost my girl and we'd lost to the arch-enemy, Liverpool. Can there be a worse place to be a Man U. fan than here in Prescot on the eastern rim of Merseyside? There are ten Scousers for every Manc round here, and every one of them's been asking me the score. I was gutted, humiliated. Now, just a few days later, I can hold my head up, and it's all down to the Reds, returning the love.

'Sure you're not coming tonight? Emma's got a couple of mates . . .'

I wrinkle my nose.

'Nah, don't feel like it.'

'It's your funeral. I'll give you a ring tomorrow.'

'Yes, see you Bobby.'

He bumps into Mum and Amy at the front door. I hear them talking.

'Why don't you go to that party?' asks Mum, emptying the shopping bags. 'It'll do you good.'

'I don't want to, OK?'

Mum holds her hands up.

'Only asking. I still don't know why you had to finish with Chloe. She's such a lovely girl.'

Chloe Blackburn, my first girlfriend. In fact, the only one so far. Yes, she is a lovely girl. But she wasn't Julie.

'You know why,' I retort. 'I like somebody else.'

'Who?'

'Julie Carter.'

'You're a silly lad,' says Mum. 'It's obvious this Julie's not interested.'

But that's the thing, Mum, she *is* interested. I can't quite believe it, but she's got feelings for me too. She told me so only last week. What did she say? *Why didn't you tell me four months ago?* Before she went out with Fitz, that is.

I had hope for us then, real hope. Then something happened, a stupid misunderstanding. And now she's back with Fitz, lousy, smirking Fitz. Plastic Scouser Fitz.

'Mum, it's my life.'

That's right, it's my life, and I'll cock it up my own way.

Tuesday 26th December
12.40 p.m.

If that's Christmas, you can keep it.

It was the tale of two turkeys, three if you count my Dad. I had Christmas dinner with Mum and Amy and gran and grandad Thompson. The turkey was moist, the sprouts were firm and my thoughts were elsewhere . . . with Julie, where else?

Is she with Fitz? Is she happy?

I had Christmas tea with Dad and Amy in his scabby flat. The turkey was burnt and the sprouts had dissolved into a green mush, so we had TV dinners on our knees and I was still thinking about Julie.

Do they have mistletoe? Are they kissing?

That was Christmas Day. It came, it went, it was rubbish. Still, at least life's half-way back to normal now. There's a full football programme today. Arsenal have already kicked off. They're 1–0 up against Leicester through Henry. I suck in my breath. If they run out winners, we've got to beat Villa away to keep our eight-point lead at the top.

'Oh, it's not football again,' moans Amy, walking into the living room.

My little sister doesn't understand the beautiful game.

'I'm afraid so.'

'I wish you and Dad still went to the match,' she says.

You and me both, Amy. My season ticket was a victim of Mum and Dad's separation. Family finances just don't run to it any more. I have to make do with Sky Sports instead. The Villa–United game starts with relentless United pressure.

Giggs, Solskjaer and Butt all have good chances. After twenty minutes we've had sixty per cent of possession, but it's still 0–0.

Zero progress, like Julie and me.

At Highbury Arsenal are running away with it. They're 3–1 up. At Villa Park, Paul Scholes goes close with a header. Another newsflash from Highbury. Now its 4–1. The pressure is on us to come up with a goal. We reach half-time. United's possession stands at seventy per cent, astonishing for the away team, but no breakthrough.

Same as Julie and me.

Meanwhile, the news from Highbury has got even worse. Arsenal have battered Leicester 6–1. I'm on the edge of my seat, willing the Reds to score, but as the minutes go by I'm becoming more and more tense. All that possession and nothing to show for it. Beckham's crosses don't have the usual zip, Ole Solskjaer's killer instinct seems to have deserted him.

'Come on, lads.'

Six minutes to go and I'm losing hope.

Then the breakthrough comes. Beckham crosses, Solskjaer scores with a sweet header. How could I have doubted them?

Villa 0 United 1.

We've broken their unbeaten home record and hung on to our eight point lead. Suddenly, it dawns on me, there's a lesson in this, Terry lad. United haven't had it easy all this season. We got turned over by Chelsea in the Charity Shield. We lost to Arsenal and Liverpool, but did we fold? Did we heck! We had that bit of steel. Keep your nerve, hold on to what you know to be true and things are bound to turn out all right in the end. Keep your nerve, that's it! I've done enough chasing round after Julie. That's right, who wants somebody who acts all forlorn and needy?

I'm not going to be a little, lovesick puppy any more, trailing round after her, embarrassing myself. The lovelorn bit hasn't worked, so I've got to change tack. I'm going to salvage some dignity. I'll take a leaf out of United's book. What I need is tactics, a strategy. I'm going to play it cool. Wouldn't that be a novelty? No matter how often she glances round, she won't catch me looking at her soulfully. No matter how much I'm tempted, I'll be looking the other way.

Thursday 28th December
8.30 a.m.

I'm woken by Amy squealing her head off. Her best friend Katie slept over last night and she's squealing too.

'Mum, Terry, come and look. It snowed in the night.'

I stagger to the window in my boxer shorts. Amy's right. It's a total white-out. Everywhere's covered in a blanket of snow, two or three inches at least. I watch for a few moments then climb back into bed. My mind starts playing a game of What Ifs.

What if you could win the Double or win Julie? Which would you choose?

What if you could get Mum and Dad back together or win Julie? What then?

I shake my head. Even if life was like that, how could I make such a choice?

But what if life turned out the way it ought to? Me and Julie together, United winning the Premiership and the Champions' League, Dad back where he belongs, that would be my idea of heaven on Earth. The trill of my mobile breaks in on my thoughts.

'Hello?'

'You up yet, misery guts?'

It's Bobby. I didn't think he knew half past eight existed!

'Get up, you lazy dog.'

This is Bobby calling me lazy! We're talking pots, kettles and the colour black.

'I'm calling for Emma on my way to yours,' he says. 'You're going to enjoy yourself, and that's an order. Snowtime!'

'But . . .'

It's too late to tell him I'd rather stay in and feel sorry for myself. He's already hung up.

'Terry love,' Mum calls, 'Would you take Amy and Katie to the park? They're really excited.'

'But I was going out with Bobby.'

'Where?'

'Snowball fight.'

'Perfect. You can take the girls with you.'

Her voice changes. She's obviously talking to Amy and Katie.

'Terry will take you to the park.'

The announcement is met with deafening cheers.

Thursday 28th December
10.00 a.m.

'I know,' shouts Bobby. 'Snow angels.'

He throws himself on his back, flapping his arms to make wings in the snow. Before I know it, Emma, Amy and Katie have joined him, laughing like mad things.

'Come in and join us, Terry. The snow's lovely.'

Oh well, in for a penny, in for a pound. I flop down, flapping my arms.

I take my eyes off the others just long enough for them to pound me with snowballs.

'Right,' I declare, clawing up handfuls of snow, 'You're dead.'

Within moments I'm in the thick of a furious snowball fight. My ears and cheeks are burning with the cold and slowly melting snow is running down my back, but I couldn't care less. I'm having fun.

'Who wants to help me build a snowman?' asks Emma.

Amy and Katie are jumping up and down, shouting: 'Me, me!'

'She's good with them,' I say, watching Emma organising the girls.

'Yes, she's great,' says Bobby approvingly.

'Are you going to do the right thing by this one?' I ask.

'Meaning?'

I'm thinking about his exes, Caitlin and Rosie.

'No two-timing her.'

Bobby winks.

'You never know, Terry lad, you never know.'

He jogs over to help with the snowman. I shake my head. The sun's come out and it's gleaming on the spire of Prescot parish church in the distance. It's a picture postcard scene. A gang of lads are playing football. My thoughts go back three weeks to footy practice. At half past three that Wednesday afternoon Julie had all but told me she was going to dump Fitz. By half past four my hopes were dashed. And all because of a stupid misunderstanding. I close my eyes and I'm there on the pitch. Fitz is goading me: *You'll never take my place in this team. You are the weakest link.* We go for a fifty-fifty ball. He's got his studs up. *You are the weakest link, goodbye.* I refuse to pull out. I will not back down. There's a sickening crunch, then a loud scream. It's Fitz. I've broken his ankle.

It was an accident Julie, an accident.

But she'll never believe that now. And that's why she's with him, because he's a victim, and I'm a thug.

But it wasn't like that, Julie. It wasn't like that at all.

'Hey Terry,' shouts Bobby, 'Get over here. You don't think you're leaving all the hard work to us, do you?'

I smile and join in. As if by magic, Bobby has produced a carrot for the snowman's nose and a couple of two-pence pieces for the eyes when I hear familiar voices. Kelly Magee and Gary Tudor, Fitz and . . . Julie. The four of them are pretty much inseparable.

Gary's the first to say anything: 'Well, if it isn't Chopper Payne.'

194

I scowl.

'It was an accident, Gary.'

'Yes, sure it was. You're such a little innocent, just like Roy Keane.'

Fitz lets his mate do the talking. He stands propped up on his crutches, enjoying my discomfort. He's clever like that. He knows the best way to Julie's heart is to play the victim. And, boy, doesn't he milk it! Look at him, all blue eyes and Michael Owen haircut – you'd think butter wouldn't melt in his mouth. I can feel Julie's eyes on me, but I refuse to meet them, even though it's killing me. These new tactics, I never thought they'd be so tough to put into action.

As they turn to go, Fitz stumbles. Julie puts an arm round his waist to support him.

'He did that on purpose,' says Bobby, 'For your benefit.'

'Tell me something I don't know,' I say.

'Move on,' says Bobby. 'You're flogging a dead horse.'

I watch Julie and Fitz crossing the park. Now that she's got her back to me, it's safe to look. Flogging a dead horse? Maybe. All these months and I'm no closer to taking her out.

But I can still remember her words before the practice match when it all went wrong: *If only you'd told me four months ago.* And she kissed me. I'm not imagining it. It happened. I can still feel the press of her lips on mine. That sort of feeling doesn't just vanish because of a misunderstanding.

There's something there. I know there is. Fitz isn't right for you, Julie. You're not happy with him. If only I could talk to you alone, just for a few minutes, if only I could explain. But I won't plead and I won't beg. I'm not going to run after you, Julie Carter. I've got my pride. No matter how hard it is, every time I see you I'm not going to give myself away.

Sunday 31st December
10.30 p.m.

I knew this was a mistake. I knew it the moment Bobby persuaded me into it. Going to a New Year's party in my frame of mind. Am I mad? For starters, the moment we arrived Bobby left me on my own, to dance with Emma. Then my ex,

Chloe, showed up with Jamie Sneddon. Every time I turn round, she's there with him. I think she's trying to tell me what I'm missing. As if I haven't suffered enough, Fitz has just arrived with Julie. I might have guessed they'd be here. I'm sticking to my promise though. Every time I come near Julie I'm Mr Cool, at least on the outside. I said I wouldn't go trailing after her, and I'm not. So here I am sitting on my own in a corner watching everybody else either dancing or copping off. Whoever said you never feel so lonely as when you're in the middle of the crowd got it dead right. I become aware of somebody talking to me:

'You haven't seen Bobby, have you Terry?'

It's Emma.

'No, I thought he was with you.'

'He was. I got talking to one of my mates and he just disappeared.'

Oh oh, no Bobby, you wouldn't.

'I've been all round the house looking for him.'

Not right under her nose. Bobby, you wouldn't.

'He's probably just in the loo.'

Emma smiles thinly. I think she's got an inkling.

'Yes, maybe.'

That's when I hear pandemonium in the kitchen.

Please, not Bobby.

A voice rasps over the beat of the CD player:

'I'll have you, Quinn. Outside, now!'

It's Paul Scully. He's lashing out at somebody, or at least trying to. Gary Tudor's pulling him back. That's when I see Bobby. He's got a red mark above one eye, and he's looking a bit embarrassed. Paul's still trying to get at him.

'Snogging my bird, the dirty little get.'

I catch sight of Pepsey Cooper, Paul's girlfriend. She looks upset, you know, caught-at-it upset. Her mascara's running. Bobby, you idiot. Right under Emma's nose, and Paul's. Talk about asking for it. Paul gets a hand free and thumps Bobby smack on the nose. It takes Gary and a couple of other lads to restrain him. I glance round at Emma. Her eyes are welling up. Oh great! Now I'm going to have to take care of her. She turns and heads for the door.

'Emma!'

I glare at Bobby. This was bound to happen some time. I'm about to follow Emma when I come face to face with Julie. Am I mistaken, or is she following me round? I'm tempted to speak to her. My God, are the tactics working? Great, here's Julie pursuing *me* and I've got my arms full with Emma. Aaargh!

'Emma, you can't go home alone, not when you're upset.'

Even as I'm saying it, I'm actually hoping she can. She looks at me.

'How could he do that to me, Terry? How?'

I notice Julie standing on the doorstep, watching us. What do I do? I just want to dump Emma and run to Julie. But Emma's suffering. Bobby's done the dirty on her and she needs a friend. That's what I'm good at, being a friend. This is killing me, Julie, just killing me. I take Emma's arm and lead her away.

'Come on, Emma, I'll walk you home.'

What am I, some sort of rotten saint? Emma smiles.

'You're a nice guy, Terry.'

Yes, that's me, nice guy, but you know what they say about nice guys? They never get the girls. Emma kisses me on the cheek. My face starts to burn. What if Julie saw us? What if she takes it wrong? As Emma and I walk off down the street, I'm dying to know if Julie's still watching. Did she want to talk to me? And what about? But I don't look back. I'm not going to chase after her like a lovesick kid. I'm doing the right thing. I know I am.

Aren't I?

Monday 1st January 2001
A minute past midnight

I'm on my own again. I have been since eleven o'clock. Emma and I were just turning into her street when Bobby came panting up. It was all a mistake, he said, a misunderstanding. Just let me explain. And Emma let him. That's how I left them, with Bobby in grovel mode and Emma slowly thawing. He'll win her round. That's what he does, Bobby. He charms people.

Since then I've been wandering round, killing time. I must

have relived every moment of my pursuit of Julie, my first sight of her in the school gym, the time she got together with Fitz at the school disco, the time she kissed me. I told Mum I'd be home by half past midnight. See in the New Year and come straight home. So I wasn't about to turn up an hour and a half early. I don't want her thinking I'm a loser.

Which I suppose I am. Especially if Julie thought Emma and I . . . It's nagging at me. Not another misunderstanding. I mean, that's two to explain, and I'm no Bobby. I don't do charm. It's a relief to see the fireworks and hear the strains of Auld Lang Syne. Now I can head home and put a brave face on the disastrous evening. I turn into our street and groan.

It's Dad. He's rotten drunk and he's shouting his head off:

'Just give me another chance, Sharon. I love you.'

Except it comes out *Ahlurrvya*.

He says it over and over again:

Ahlurrvya, ahlurrvya, ahlurrvya.

Then he sinks to his knees on the pavement.

Oh Dad!

All the neighbours are looking. Mum's at the window too.

'Terry, would you get him out of here?'

'Dad, get up,' I plead. 'I'll take you home.'

'But I love her,' he says.

It comes out *Ahlurrverr*.

Ahlurrverr, ahrlurrverr, ahlurrverr.

'I know you do, Dad,' I say, guiding him in the direction of his flat. 'But this isn't the way to show it.'

'Then what is, Terry?'

As we stagger away I lift my eyes to the sky. I remember Emma kissing me on the cheek. Then I think of the way I ignored Julie. It seems a good idea at the time. Now I'm not so sure.

'Tell me, Terry, what is the way to show it?'

I have to give him an honest reply.

'I don't know, Dad. I just don't know.'

Also by Alan Gibbons

THE LEGENDEER TRILOGY

The Shadow of the Minotaur

'Real life' or the death defying adventures of the Greek myths, with their heroes and monsters, daring deeds and narrow escapes – which would you choose?

For Phoenix it's easy. He hates his new home and the new school where he is bullied. He's embarrassed by his computer geek dad. But when he logs on to the Legendeer, the game his dad is working on, he can be a hero. He is Theseus fighting the terrifying Minotaur, or Perseus battling with snake-haired Medusa.

The trouble is The Legendeer is more than just a game. Play it if you dare.

Vampyr Legion

What if there are real worlds where our nightmares live and wait for us?

Phoenix has found one and it's alive. Armies of bloodsucking vampyrs and terrifying werewolves, the creatures of our darkest dreams, are posed to invade our world.

But Phoenix has encountered the creator of *Vampyr Legion*, the evil Gamesmaster, before and knows that this deadly computer game is for real – he must win or never come back.

Warriors of the Raven

The game opens up the gateway between our world and the world of the myths.

The Gamesmaster almost has our world at his mercy. Twice before fourteen-year-old Phoenix has battled against him in *Shadow of the Minotaur* and *Vampyr Legion*, but *Warriors of the Raven* is the game at its most complex and deadly level. This time, Phoenix enters the arena for the final conflict, set in the world of Norse myth. Join Phoenix in Asgard to fight Loki, the Mischief-maker, the terrifying Valkyries, dragons and fire demons – and hope for victory. Our future depends on him.

Whose Side Are You On

SOME THINGS ARE WORTH FIGHTING FOR . . .

Mattie likes a quiet life. When the school bullies start picking on his Asian friend, Pravin, he knows he should do something about it. Too scared to act, Mattie runs away. But instead of escaping, somehow he is transported to the very heart of slavery, a sugar plantation in eighteenth-century Jamaica, not knowing whether he will return home . . .

A powerful and compelling novel.